MIDDLEMARCH

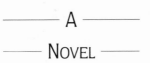

A

NOVEL

OF

REFORM

MIDDLEMARCH

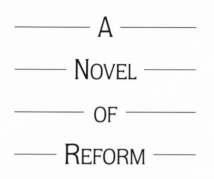

A
NOVEL
OF
REFORM

BERT G. HORNBACK

TWAYNE PUBLISHERS • BOSTON
A Division of G. K. Hall & Co.

MIDDLEMARCH: A NOVEL OF REFORM
BERT G. HORNBACK

Twayne's Masterwork Studies No. 14

Book Production by Gabrielle B. McDonald
Copyediting supervised by Barbara Sutton
Typeset in 10/14 Sabon
by Compset, Inc., of Beverly, Massachusetts

Printed on permanent/durable acid-free paper
and bound in the United States of America

Library of Congress Cataloging-in-Publication Data

Hornback, Bert G., 1935–
Middlemarch : a novel of reform / Bert G. Hornback.
p.   cm.—(Twayne's masterwork studies ; no. 14)
Bibliography: p.
Includes index.
ISBN 0-8057-7981-7.   ISBN 0-8057-8031-9 (pbk.)
1. Eliot, George, 1819–1880. Middlemarch.   I. Title.
II. Series.
PR4662.H67   1988
823'.8—dc19

In memory of
Nancy Ruth Wicker

Contents

Note on References and Acknowledgments

All references to *Middlemarch* in this book are to the *Norton Critical Edition of Middlemarch*, which is based on the 1874 edition and incorporates George Eliot's revisions.

I have been teaching *Middlemarch* for many years and am grateful to all the students who have studied it with me, and most especially to the students in my once-a-week *Middlemarch* mini-course at The University of Michigan, who heard an early version of this book in the form of lectures. They listened critically and responded in writing at the end of class each week. A selection from their responses appears at the end of this book.

I also wish to thank Joseph Duffy, who first taught me *Middlemarch*. Tish O'Dowd Ezekiel, Dorothy Foster, Brendan Mahaney, and Zibby Oneal have read my manuscript and have helped me with their generous suggestions, corrections, and understandings. They did not always agree with me—nor will you, I suspect.

I have represented earlier critics and our contemporaries as fairly as I could, and I have tried in what I have written about their work to give an account of readings of *Middlemarch* different from my own. In what I have said about the novel I have tried always to keep my focus on what I believe to be George Eliot's chief concern, that art be involved with her readers' real lives.

Bert G. Hornback
University of Michigan

George Eliot (Mary Anne Evans)
1819–1880
Courtesy of National Portrait Gallery, London.

Chronology: George Eliot's Life and Works

1819	Mary Anne Evans born 22 November at South Farm, Arbury, Warwickshire, the third child of Robert and Christiana Evans.
1824	Attends Mrs. Moore's school in Griff and is later a boarder to Miss Lathom's school in Attleborough.
1828	Attends Mrs. Wallington's school in Nuneaton, where she meets Maria Lewis, her favorite teacher and an important influence on her early life.
1836	Mother dies.
1840	First poem, "Farewell," published in the *Christian Observer*.
1841	Moves with her father to Foleshill, and reads Charles Hennell's *An Inquiry Concerning the Origin of Christianity*.
1843	Reads Spinoza.
1844	Begins translation of Strauss's *Das Leben Jesu*.
1846	*The Life of Jesus* published.
1849	Father dies.
1851	Goes to London as assistant editor of the *Westminster Review*.
1853	Meets George Henry Lewes.
1854	Translation of Feuerbach's *The Essence of Christianity* published. She and Lewes leave for Germany together, traveling as husband and wife.
1856	Finishes translating Spinoza's *Ethics* and begins to write "Amos Barton," a short story.
1857	"Amos Barton" published, anonymously. Assumes the George Eliot pseudonym and begins *Adam Bede*.
1858	*Scenes of Clerical Life*—including "Amos Barton"—published.
1859	*Adam Bede* published. Reveals her identity as George Eliot.
1860	*The Mill on the Floss* published.

1861	*Silas Marner* published.
1862	*Romola* begins serial publications in *Cornhill Magazine*.
1863	*Romola* completed and published in book form.
1866	*Felix Holt* published.
1868	*The Spanish Gipsy*, a long dramatic poem, published.
1869	Begins *Middlemarch*. She and Lewes meet John Cross (b. 1840), whom they befriend.
1870	Meets Dante Gabriel Rossetti.
1871	Book 1 of *Middlemarch* published in December.
1872	*Middlemarch* concludes in December. *Wise, Witty, and Tender Sayings of George Eliot* published.
1874	*The Legend of Jubal and Other Poems* published.
1876	*Daniel Deronda* published.
1878	Lewes dies 30 November; John Cross's mother dies on 9 December.
1879	Begins seeing Cross frequently.
1880	Marries Cross on 6 May. They go to Venice on their honeymoon but return to England on 26 July. On 3 December they move to 4 Cheyne Walk in London. On 22 December George Eliot dies.
1885	Cross publishes *George Eliot's Life as Related in her Letters and Journals*.
1924	John Cross dies.

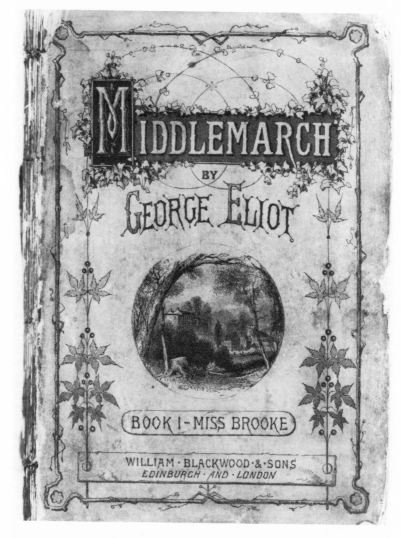

Cover of the original serial edition of *Middlemarch*.

• 1 •

HISTORICAL CONTEXT

Mary Anne Evans was born in the same year as Alexandrina Victoria, the daughter of the Duke and Duchess of Kent. In 1837 Victoria became queen of England, and ruled—as queen, defender of the faith, and empress—until 1901. British history has given those sixty-four years her name, calling them the Victorian age. Mary Anne Evans grew up into the Victorian age, and records in her life and in her work many of the critical issues of its early and middle years.

As a young woman, Mary Anne Evans was an evangelical Christian, believing in the fundamentalist doctrine of salvation by faith alone. By the time she was twenty-five she had become exposed to that radical questioning of Christianity which was known as "the higher criticism."[1] In 1842 she wrote to her father concerning "the Christian Scriptures" that they are "histories consisting of mingled truth and fiction." While she could "admire and cherish . . . the moral teaching of Jesus himself," she rejected Christianity's "system of doctrines" as "most dishonourable to God and most pernicious in its influence on individual and social happiness."[2]

In 1843 she read Spinoza's rationalist arguments about Christianity and ethics, and the next year set out to translate David Friedrich Strauss's *Das Leben Jesu*. Strauss's work was perhaps the single most important book on Christianity to appear in the nineteenth century; rejecting the supernatural or divine in Christ's life, it became the bible for the school of the higher criticism. Mary Anne Evans's translation was published, anonymously, in 1846.

As the attacks on traditional Christian faith increased in number and grew stronger in their effect, many people searched for a substitute for lost order and security. To some that substitute was the ideal of material "Progress": new wealth, new inventions, new opportunities. Empire abroad and Benthamite liberalism at home became their new religion. To others, the failure of Christian doctrine left—as it did for George Eliot—Christian ideas and principles, upon which the individual now had to build a new moral order. If the world were not God's world, ordered by divine intervention, then it must be our world, for which we must assume responsibility. Those who believed in Progress accepted Thomas Babington Macaulay as the new prophet; according to his gospel, the improvement of the nation and the general good of the world would result from "leaving capital to find its most lucrative course, commodities their fair price, industry and intelligence their natural reward, idleness and folly their natural punishment."[3] Those who could not trust the new capitalistic ethic as a replacement for divine order became, in the midst of Victorian prosperity, its social critics.

The Victorian age meant a combination of huge success for those who ruled the material world and terrible misery for those whose labor enabled that success. The miserable masses were for the most part unheard from. Though there were rick-burnings on farms and machine-breakings in factories in the first decades of the century, and in early Victorian times the angry uprisings of the Chartists and the trades unionists, Britain never came close to popular revolution in the nineteenth century, in large part because Victorian social critics became a genuine force in their society. Despite the claims of the materialist gospel of Progress, Britain created a new, modern, humane conscience for itself.

Historical Context

The most striking emblem of Progress was the Crystal Palace, built to house The Great Exhibition of 1851. Prince Albert, Victoria's consort, was its inspiration and patron, and chose for its motto the biblical motif, "The Earth is the Lord's and all that therein is."[4] Shimmering grandly in Hyde Park, this great glass cathedral was also an emblem for the other side of Victorianism. In its self-confidence, Progress indeed exhibited itself—and its critics took advantage of the crystal transparency of that exhibition.

The major social critics of the Victorian age included intellectuals like John Stuart Mill, Matthew Arnold, and John Ruskin—and novelists like Charles Dickens, Benjamin Disraeli, and George Eliot. The young woman who translated Strauss's *Leben Jesu* in 1846 went on to translate Ludwig Feuerbach's equally radical *Essence of Christianity* in 1854, and then became, in 1857—as a writer of fiction—George Eliot.

By the time of *Middlemarch*, her sixth novel, George Eliot was well established as both an intellectual and a novelist. She was generally known, by then, to be Mary Anne—or, as she sometimes signed herself, Marian—Evans. She was not married, though from 1854 on she and George Henry Lewes lived together as husband and wife. Lewes was one of the most accomplished and versatile intellectuals of the time. He was one of the founders of the *Leader,* a radical newspaper, and the editor of several different influential journals. His most important works, however, were his *Life of Goethe,* published in 1855, and his advice and assistance to George Eliot. Though initially there were many Victorians who were outraged by George Eliot's action in living with Lewes, by the time of *Middlemarch* she was fully accepted by society, and entertained even the Queen's daughters.

All of this—religion, progress, social criticism, intellectual life, manners and morals, women's roles in the world—is important as background for *Middlemarch*. One more item has to be included, however, before our historical setting for the novel is complete. In 1867, Parliament passed what was known as the Second Great Reform Bill. Reform—"the Rinform" to farmer Dagley in *Middlemarch*—had been an almost constant issue in Britain since the 1820s.

The Reform Bill of 1832 had made great changes in British life, enlarging the franchise and revising the composition of Parliament. In 1838 the Chartists demanded universal male suffrage and further parliamentary reforms; in the 1840s the trades union movement demanded—and won—improvements in working conditions in the mines and factories. By 1860 it was clear that further reform was necessary, but the establishment was uneasy about how such change would affect English society. The Second Great Reform Bill was still a matter of concern four years after its passage, when *Middlemarch* began to appear in bi-monthly installments.

Middlemarch was not set in contemporary time, however. It opens in 1829, and works its way forward in history only as far as the passage of the Reform Bill of 1832. But it is a novel insistently concerned with reform, so that in its theme it was a contemporary novel for its first readers. As we have not yet managed to perfect either our society or this world—and both thus are still in need of considerable reform—it should be a contemporary novel for us as well.

Though *Middlemarch* is set in the years shortly before Victoria's accession to the throne, it is for many readers the greatest of the Victorian novels. And for many others, though it was written at the midpoint of Victoria's long reign, *Middlemarch* stands as the first great modern novel.

• 2 •

THE IMPORTANCE OF THE WORK

Middlemarch is the sixth of George Eliot's seven novels, and her greatest achievement as a writer. Others of her novels remain popular—*Adam Bede* (1859), *The Mill on the Floss* (1860), perhaps *Silas Marner* (1861)—and her translations of Strauss and Feuerbach were important contributions to the intellectual life of her times. But *Middlemarch* stands alone among her works, and in a very select company, as one of the greatest works of English literature.

Middlemarch is remarkable for its richness, its variety, its scope, its technique, and its ideas. We know a great deal about the kind of novel it will be from the opening sentence of the Prelude: "Who that cares much to know the history of man, and how the mysterious mixture behaves under the varying experiments of Time, has not dwelt, at least briefly, on the life of Saint Theresa, has not smiled with some gentleness at the thought of the little girl walking forth one morning . . ." (xiii). Our subject—the subject George Eliot expects us to be interested in—is "the history of man." She assumes that her audience "cares . . . to know" this history, and seems to indicate that our approach should be almost scientific: knowledge of human history and existence comes from watching "how the mysterious mixture be-haves" in various "experiments." This watching, however, is not just a matter of simple observation. It is contemplative, meditative; and George Eliot leads us to "dwell, at least briefly," upon "the life of Saint Theresa," the sixteenth-century Spanish mystic who was one of the most remarkable women in all of history.

But Saint Theresa is introduced to us, not in her glory, but as a "little girl . . . wide-eyed and helpless looking." She is not an ordinary little girl, however; despite the "uncles" who would advise, protect, and restrain her, Theresa's "passionate, ideal nature demand[s] an epic life." She grows up seeking "some object [in life] which would never justify weariness." She finds her greatness in "life beyond self," and in "the reform of a religious order" (xiii).

Though the Prelude to *Middlemarch* does introduce us primarily to Dorothea Brooke, the heroine of the novel, it does so in an inclusive rather than an exclusive way. Saint Theresa enters the world much as Dorothea will enter her world, which is Middlemarch. Saint Theresa is "wide-eyed" in her innocence—as is Dorothea, metaphorically. Lit-erally, however, Dorothea is a bit old for wide-eyed innocence; she is already a young woman, not a little girl. And since she is myopic, she should perhaps squint a little, in order to see her world better, more clearly.

The significant word that George Eliot chooses to describe both Saint Theresa and Dorothea, in their anxious yearnings after "spiritual grandeur," is "ardour." In its repetition throughout the novel this word becomes a kind of thought-image for the passion for meaningful life that burns in Dorothea and eventually enlightens—or should en-lighten—this world.

There are those in the story, of course, who won't take Dorothea seriously—some simply because she is a woman, others because her idealism can only cause trouble in a time that has "no coherent faith and order" to guide it. In this modern world women like Dorothea, with her "ardently willing soul" demanding a "life beyond self," can no longer find their satisfaction in reforming religious orders; if unchecked by avuncular wisdom, they are likely to invade other institutions and question our whole modern way of life.

George Eliot is a realist, and recognizes the power of "uncles." She does not propose to us, in the Prelude or in *Middlemarch* itself, that Dorothea will change the world. But if we take the novel seriously—if we are serious about "the history of man"—we may ourselves be changed. As an artist, George Eliot was ambitious in a most serious way: she believed that art could change our lives, by "enlarg[ing] our sympathies."[5] Perhaps it is this seriousness of purpose which made Virginia Woolf call *Middlemarch* "one of the few English novels written for grown-up people"[6]—if indeed grown-up people take life seriously!

· 3 ·

CRITICAL RECEPTION

Virginia Woolf's appreciation of *Middlemarch* is one of the most famous critical judgments in the history of English literary criticism. That *Middlemarch* is a novel "for grown-up people"[7] is not such an odd thing to say about it: indeed, Woolf echoes many of George Eliot's earliest critics, who lacked the verbal skill to say the thing in such plain words. But until Virginia Woolf's time, most of George Eliot's critics matched their appreciation of the mature seriousness of *Middlemarch* with complaints about its moral argument. The *Saturday Review,* for example, found that "Never before have so keen and varied an observation, so strong a grasp of conceptions, such power of picturesque description worked together to represent through the agency of fiction an author's moral and social views." To the reviewer, *Middlemarch* "as a didactic novel . . . has scarcely been equalled." But both George Eliot's didacticism and its point are unacceptable: the reviewer complains of George Eliot's prejudice against "the ordinary domestic type of woman" such as Celia and Rosamond, whom "we are not allowed to find . . . attractive." If "our young ladies . . . take to be Dorotheas," he concludes, "the world will be a less comfortable world without being a better one."[8]

Sidney Colvin, writing for the *Fortnightly Review,* is not so defensive. He writes of George Eliot's "modern analytic mind" as at once a "psychological instrument" by which she probes with "sympathetic insight into the workings of human nature" and a "scientific" or otherwise critical "instrument," "something like a medical habit in the writer," by which she "examin[es] her own creations for their symptoms." To Colvin, "nothing in the literature of the day is so rousing" as *Middlemarch*; "every word bites with peculiar sharpness to the contemporary consciousness."[9]

To Henry James, *Middlemarch* is "at once one of the strongest and one of the weakest of English novels." "It sets a limit," he says, "to the development of the old-fashioned English novel." But it is terribly "old-fashioned," as James reads it, "a treasure-house of details, but . . . an indifferent whole." James likes George Eliot's creation of Lydgate and Rosamond, and admires Dorothea's "affect" as "the greatest achievement of the book." Will, however, is unsatisfactory, a mere "*dilettante*" in spite of George Eliot's efforts to make him more than that. A "masculine intellect" would have created Will more successfully.[10]

Edith Simcox praises *Middlemarch* where James finds fault—for its "artistic harmony of construction." It "marks an epoch in the history of fiction," she claims, "in so far as its incidents are taken from inner life" and "the action is developed by the direct influence of mind on mind and character on character." *Middlemarch* is "a profoundly imaginative psychological study," replete with "perfect realistic truth." To Simcox, however, this "truth" is that of "two rather sad fatalities," Lydgate's and Dorothea's. Their "failures" are "irrevocably necessary," she says. Lydgate's failure is pathetic: as George Eliot comments, "if we had been greater, circumstances would have been less strong against us." Dorothea's failure is what Simcox calls "tragical," because "the fault in her case seems to be altogether in the nature and constitution of the universe"—and because "for a perfect woman any marriage is a *mésalliance.*"[11]

Later critics pick up many of these early observations and enlarge upon them. Joseph Jacobs, referring to the philosophical, didactic strain in George Eliot's writing, calls her an "ethical rather than psychological" artist, interested more in "morality" than in anything else: "her whole work is imbued with ethical notions," and is "a criticism of life." Jacobs also praises her "impartiality," and her generous "extension of sympathy" to all her characters.[12] Leslie Stephen respects George Eliot's "reflective powers" but objects that in *Middlemarch*, for all the strength of her creation, George Eliot is "a little out of touch with the actual world" and "rather too much impressed by the importance of philosophers and theorists." To Stephen's cynical mind, the world "worries along by means of very commonplace affections and very limited outlooks"; he supposes that George Eliot "fully recognizes that fact" but is "dispirited" by its "contemplation"—and thus creates Dorothea. In response to Dorothea, Stephen "can only comfort [him]self by reflecting that, after all, she had a dash of stupidity, and that more successful Theresas may do a good deal of mischief."[13]

In our time we have grown somewhat less defensive about George Eliot and *Middlemarch* and Dorothea. Virginia Woolf—Leslie Stephen's daughter—leads us in praising both George Eliot and her work freely. Her appreciation of *Middlemarch* as "the magnificent book which with all its imperfections is one of the few English novels written for grown-up people" comes from her respect for George Eliot the woman. For Virginia Woolf "the facts of human existence" dictate Dorothea's frustration at the end of *Middlemarch;* but Dorothea's story is only "the incomplete version of the story of George Eliot herself," who in her "triumphant" life "sought more knowledge and more freedom till the body . . . sank worn out."[14]

Lord David Cecil compliments George Eliot for her "grip on psychological essentials," and finds her "concentration on the moral side of human nature . . . the kernel of her precious unique contribution to our literature." But he doesn't find much satisfaction in the conclusion to *Middlemarch:* "Desperately [George Eliot] reiterates the articles of her creed, anxiously tries to convince us that Dorothea's unselfish devotion to husband and children made up for her failure to realize her youthful dreams. But she does not even convince herself. . . . Dorothea's life leaves her disappointed, disheartened and depressed. And she communicates her depression to her readers."[15] Mimicking Leslie Stephen, F. R. Leavis praises George Eliot's "great intellectual powers," but then complains of the "abeyance of intelligence and self-knowledge" evident in her creation of Dorothea. Elsewhere George Eliot's "sheer informedness" is "knowledge alive with understanding," her characters created out of "intelligence lighted by compassion." But Dorothea, "all-comprehending and irresistibly good," exists as but "a product of George Eliot's own 'soul-hunger'—another day-dream ideal self." At odds with George Eliot's notion of the purpose of art, Leavis glories in Rosamond, "wanting to break that graceful neck," but rejects Dorothea's beauty as "indulgence . . . generated by a need to soar above the indocile facts and conditions of the real world."[16]

Middlemarch seems to demand of its readers a personal response—and this demand is perhaps proof of its success, in George Eliot's terms. Over and over its critics declare themselves, as believers or nonbelievers. It is at least remarkable—if not tellingly odd—that so many men find George Eliot's heroine unbelievable, whereas many women become intensely involved in her life as though it were the real life of a sister. Not all women readers of the novel agree with Dorothea, or with her creator's attitude toward her; but few of them defend themselves from her the way men do, by denying her reality.

Both George Eliot and *Middlemarch* have been important to feminist studies of literature ever since Edith Simcox reviewed the novel in 1873. Virginia Woolf has been succeeded, however, by critics like Lee R. Edwards, who echoes Simcox in objecting that it "is not that Dorothea should have married Will but that she should have married anybody at all." For Edwards, George Eliot submits Dorothea to a conventional life in the end. "Dorothea is a character who might have been fulfilled in a wider world than the one [her] author finally provides"; but "looking outward, George Eliot simply could not find this new and bigger world."[17] Unlike Virginia Woolf, Edwards seems to forget "the story of George Eliot herself"[18] who—as Mary Anne Evans or even as Mrs. G. H. Lewes—lived in that larger world. Elaine Show-alter writes of George Eliot's significance to other women writers in *A Literature of Their Own*. She argues that, early on, women novelists engaged in "criticism of the Eliot legend" because they "found her a troublesome and demoralizing competitor."[19] Victorian women "could not equal her, and they could see no way around her." Showalter con-cludes: "It was not until the generation of the 1890s had dramati-cally—even sensationally—redefined the role of the woman writer that Virginia Woolf could look back and see in George Eliot, not a rival, but a heroine."[20]

She is still a rival to many men—the more so perhaps because we still call her George Eliot—and her heroine is often simply unaccept-able. The most recent criticism of *Middlemarch*, however, avoids the problem by reading not George Eliot's novel but its "text." Decon-structionist and other theoretical critics have appropriated *Middle-march*, testing their ideas against it. Hillis Miller, for example, discovers in it amazing "strategies of totalisation" underlying George Eliot's text.[21] As Kerry McSweeney writes in the conclusion to his de-lightful book on *Middlemarch* in the Unwin Critical Library, such work "is excessively *engagé* and ideological, too concerned with its own premises, methods, and self-delighting excruciations, and insuf-ficiently disinterested in George Eliot's novel."[22]

A READING

• 4 •

ENLARGING OUR SYMPATHIES

When George Eliot conceived of the novel we call *Middlemarch*, in January 1869, it was only part of what we now have. In the beginning, there was to be a story about Dorothea, called "Miss Brook."[23] And there was to be a "Novel called Middlemarch." By May of 1871 the two had become one: "The work is called Middlemarch. Part I will be Miss Brooke."[24]

Middlemarch is "A Study of Provincial Life," according to its subtitle. The key word in the subtitle is "study": it identifies the novel, in a sense, as George Eliot's. The world she proposes to study is perhaps based on Coventry, a major cloth-making town in the eighteenth and early nineteenth centuries: it would be typical of George Eliot to have as background for her creation a real place that she could know well. But Middlemarch is more importantly a mythic place, and its name suggests that. Middlemarch isn't like Utopia, an ironic "no place." Rather, Middlemarch is "anyplace." The second half of its name comes from the old word for boundary or edge of a piece of land. Middlemarch, then, is the town in the figurative "middle" of this world.

Outside the town itself—adjacent to it, but not one with it or its life—are three estates: Freshitt Manor, where the Chettams live; Lowick Manor, the residence of the Reverend Edward Casaubon; and Tipton Grange, where Mr. Brooke lives with his two nieces, Dorothea and Celia.

The problem George Eliot has set for herself in determining to combine "Miss Brooke," her story about Dorothea, with the "Novel called Middlemarch" is how to join them. In prospect, at least, they are two very different books. Dorothea's story isn't in any way a part of the "Study of Provincial Life" planned for *Middlemarch*. This is clear from the Prelude—which is a prelude to Dorothea's story, and a warning of the difficulties which "Provincial Life" will pose for her when they meet.

The Prelude speaks of the ambition toward "epic" life, of noble ideals and selfless sacrifice. It prepares for the introduction of Dorothea by suggesting to us the frustrations to be met by "later-born Theresas" whose "spiritual grandeur" must be "ill-matched with the meanness of opportunity" in our modern world (xiii). The Prelude warns us not to expect any sort of triumph for Dorothea; she may be "a St. Theresa," but she may also be the "foundress of nothing," a pathetic creature whose "ardour" for the good will "tremble off and [be] dispersed among hinderances, instead of centering on some long-recognisable deed" (xiv).

When we come to the end of this wonderfully rich and expansive novel we will want to reevaluate the Prelude and our response to it. Perhaps we will find that it has misled us. By teasing our expectations for heroics it may distract us from Dorothea's principled goodness and the radiant effect such a radical life can have upon our world.

From the beginning of chapter 1, Dorothea does not belong to—is not really of—our world. Her beauty is "that kind of beauty which seems to be thrown into relief by poor dress," and needs no addition or complement. She is so exquisite that she is out of place in this place: she is like "the Blessed Virgin," as rare and impressive as "a fine quotation from the Bible,—or from one of our elder poets—in a paragraph of to-day's newspaper"(1).

Dorothea's counterpart in the novel is Rosamond Vincy, who is very much of the world and a determinedly worldly part of it. Dorothea is introduced to us as a young woman who has in her background no "yard-measuring or parcel-tying forefathers," and she and her sister "naturally regarded frippery as the ambition of a huckster's daughter" (1). When we meet Rosamond, at the end of the first book of the novel, we find that she is addicted to "frippery"; and her father, though not quite a huckster, is a "yard-measuring and parcel-tying" mercer.

Something else besides her beauty and her social station keeps Dorothea from belonging to this world. Her understanding of life is different from that of the other characters, as is the idealistic ambition that grows from that understanding. Dorothea's "spiritual ardour" and moral seriousness are such that she seems to other, "Provincial" characters almost dangerous both to her class and to the world at large. Her "love of extremes" and strange "notions" about life are such that, should she marry, she might "awaken . . . some fine morning with a new scheme for the application of her income which would interfere with political economy and the keeping of saddle-horses" (3). It is not altogether wrong, the wry and ironic narrator suggests, for a woman to have opinions; "but the great safeguard of society and of domestic life was, that opinions were not acted on." The conventional wisdom of the enclosed world in which Dorothea finds herself at the age of twenty-one says that "Sane people did what their neighbors did" (3).

It is against this code of conduct that the great movement called Reform operates. And though it is Will Ladislaw, not Dorothea, who is interested in politics, Dorothea is the great reformer. She does, in the end, act upon her opinions; and in eventually giving up her large income she defies provincial wisdom and its definition of sanity. She breaks free of this enclosed little world—and goes to London.

But London, even as the big world, is no different from Middlemarch in reality, and Dorothea finds no "epic" life there either. She is free, however, spiritually. It is in her achievement of spiritual freedom that Dorothea is George Eliot's great reformer. There is no evidence in the novel of Dorothea's changing the lives of those around her, though certainly many people are moved by her—some to acts of genuine goodness—and she is greatly admired. Dorothea is a reformer by example: and the world that she would reform, for George Eliot, is the world in which you and I live.

Dorothea is an idealist—and like all true idealists she seeks to realize her ideals in this world. At the beginning of the novel she has already set up "an infant school . . . in the village," and has a "plan" for "new cottages for the poor" (4). She thinks up "generous schemes" for the use of her money (2), and has an "eagerness to know the truths of life" (4). Her ambition leaves her little time for thoughts of love; were she to marry, it would be to serve and be taught by some great man, like Hooker, Milton, Locke, or Pascal. "The really delightful marriage," she thinks, "must be that where your husband was a sort of father, and could teach you Hebrew" (4).

Dorothea is a wonderful young woman—but she is not quite so prepared for the kind of "useful" life in this world that she wants, and George Eliot is careful to point this fact out to us. Dorothea's "ideas about marriage," the narrator says, are "very childish" (4). And though she objects to jewels as "trinkets"—and rejects "frippery" generally—in her next breath she exclaims with delight over her mother's emeralds. When she decides to keep them, George Eliot complains of the lack of "consistency" in her act.

By the end of the first chapter of *Middlemarch*, George Eliot has prepared us for Dorothea's entry into its world. Celia speaks of their "going into society" (7). We know from the opening of the novel that the narrator loves and appreciates her heroine. We see from Dorothea's acts and words and plans that she has noble ambitions. Though George Eliot has not yet introduced Dorothea's characteristic cry of wanting "to do something," we know that she desires ardently to create for herself a useful, moral life in a world much larger than Tipton Grange. That desire, together with Dorothea's "going into society," constitutes the beginning of what will become the solution to the problem of how George Eliot can integrate the story of "Miss Brooke" into the "Novel called Middlemarch."

George Eliot is a realist—and an idealist. Indeed, there's no such thing as an idealist who isn't a realist first: without realism, idealism sinks to pie-in-the-sky sentimentalism. One needs to know this world for what it is before one can try to change it into something better. Idealism signifies, in philosophical terms, a belief in some perfection or perfectibility toward which we must strive. The opposite of idealism is not realism—which is a neutral term—but cynicism, that philosophical complacency which simply accepts things as they are, or pessimism. George Eliot's idealism reflects what she calls the morality of art: "If Art does not enlarge men's sympathies, it does nothing morally."[25]

George Eliot is a moralist, then, as an artist—and an idealist. And it is as such that she loves Dorothea. She is never sentimental in her creation of Dorothea, or in her response to her. She criticizes her heroine often: she needs to correct Dorothea's errors.

For all of this seriousness, there is also delightful comedy in *Middlemarch,* and before we go on we must take note of George Eliot's humor. It is a wry kind of humor, though sometimes cumbersome and heavy-handed. It signals, regularly, the distance between her and her creation; it also defines her carefully controlled relationship with her readers. George Eliot's humor first appears in a small way in the second paragraph of the novel. She introduces Mr. Brooke as a man who "had travelled in his younger years, and . . . [had] contracted a too rambling habit of mind" (2). A more poignant version of the same kind of linguistic joke appears in her referring to Mr. Casaubon's act of abandoning himself "to the stream of feeling," and finding out "what an exceedingly shallow rill it was" (41). There is humor, too, in Celia's pet name for her sister: "Dodo," the name of the pathetic bird, now extinct, that couldn't fly.

George Eliot also generates wonderful comedy, not unlike Dickens's, through the creation of such characters as old Peter Featherstone and his family, and little Miss Henrietta Noble. We can laugh at the covetousness of the Featherstones and the Waules because it hurts then, and we enjoy Peter Featherstone's knowing but malicious disdain for them; the old miser's scorn for his greedy relations is his saving grace. Henrietta Noble's silliness is qualified by her goodness, and that goodness is underlined by her name. While we smile at her actions, we must respect her intentions, and even—in a moral sense—her judgment. Humor and comedy in George Eliot's work always have some kind of seriousness. Her conception of the world allows for comic incidents and interludes, certainly; but her concept of art requires that these be woven into the larger fabric of serious meaning. We are never allowed just to laugh at a character in *Middlemarch*. Its author requires of us as readers more than that: and the more that she requires is that serious thing she calls sympathy.

In 1856 George Eliot published an essay in the *Westminister Review* in which she cautioned "any female reader who is in danger of adding to the number of 'silly novels by lady novelists.'"[26] It would be hard to imagine George Eliot herself ever needing to be warned against silliness; from the beginning of her artistic career her serious and intellectual bent was remarked by her readers. Seriousness was natural to George Eliot. Her purpose as an artist was always didactic, though what she presumed to teach was more moral feeling than moral precept. I suspect that, like Socrates, she believed that virtue can be taught only because virtue is knowledge, or understanding, or a high and noble kind of sympathy. Thoughts and actions that are not virtuous, then, are ignorant, not simply evil. And though ignorance may be blamed, it must also be pitied.

As an intellectual, George Eliot was dedicated to the kind of knowledge that accumulates information and arranges facts. In *Middlemarch* we see this part of her most in the background of medical information that she provides for Tertius Lydgate's character. Because she kept a double notebook for *Middlemarch,* which she called her "Quarry," we can also appreciate how meticulously she collected that information.[27]

There are several intellectuals or would-be intellectuals in *Mid-*

dlemarch. Lydgate is a medical scientist. Casaubon gathers information for his scholarly *Key to All Mythologies*. Mr. Farebrother collects bugs and beetles—he is an entymologist. And Mr. Brooke collects all the odds and ends of a mock-serious life.

Mr. Brooke may stand as a mock-intellectual, but Lydgate's intellectualism and Casaubon's pretense mock their humanity. Entymology is but a hobby for Farebrother, just as whist is for him more a distraction than a vice. Lydgate and Casaubon, however, try in their different ways to construct their lives out of their intellectual endeavors. For George Eliot such activity suffices by itself neither to legitimize a life nor to create human happiness.

Dorothea is George Eliot's character in *Middlemarch*—and like her creator, Dorothea is not just an intellectual, however eager she may be to learn things, or to be taught Hebrew. Dorothea wants "to know the truths of life" (4)—and that is the rich, human ambition for which George Eliot appreciates her. Dorothea is as much George Eliot's character as Emma Woodhouse is Jane Austen's, or David Copperfield is Dickens's. At the end of *Middlemarch,* Dorothea achieves George Eliot's values, just as Emma and David achieve those of their creators. From the beginning, Dorothea is serious about things—just as George Eliot is. But at twenty-one Dorothea does not know enough—does not know as much as George Eliot does—and thus she makes mistakes sometimes.

When other characters in *Middlemarch* make mistakes, we see them suffer the consequences; if they learn through their suffering, we nod our heads in condescending congratulation, as if to say "At last!" We are studying "Provincial Life" when we look at them, and our concern with them resembles that of the observer of a scientific demonstration. When Dorothea—"Miss Brooke"—makes a mistake, George Eliot creates both the mistake and its meaning differently.

Dorothea's motives, when she falls in error, are invariably different from those of Casaubon, Lydgate, or Will Ladislaw—the other great mistake-makers in the novel—when they err. Though Lydgate's, Casaubon's, and Will's values and ambitions are not all or always bad, when they make mistakes it is because their values are wrong, and their ambitions are to serve themselves. Dorothea, however, makes her mistakes when she is trying, at least, to serve the world. And for George Eliot, serving the world is the highest, noblest ambition one can have.

When Dorothea makes a mistake we usually know the context in which she is about to act. We have seen the world as she sees it, first, and we have seen her critical understanding of it. We sympathize with that understanding, on moral grounds. But when Dorothea acts, she acts wrongly and frustrates us. She gives up riding the same way she marries Casaubon: out of ignorance. She desires ardently to serve the world, but she doesn't know enough yet about herself or the world. "She doesn't understand enough yet," we say. Like her creator, we expect her to understand more. Such understanding, after all, is what we know from the beginning the story of "Miss Brooke" must be about.

A good example of George Eliot's complex presentation of Dorothea appears in chapter 2, at the party at Mr. Brooke's attended by the Chettams and Mr. Casaubon. The chapter begins with Mr. Brooke talking his usual nonsense, and Dorothea wonders "how a man like Mr. Casaubon would support such triviality" (8). Casaubon, we soon learn, is a man composed of trivialities; unlike Brooke's, however, Casaubon's are trivialities enhanced and engorged by the egotism of one who "feed[s] too much on the inward sources" (9). But Dorothea is blinded to Casaubon—she thinks he resembles Locke—and to everything else in the scene. And Dorothea's blindness is itself a kind of egotism: she sees what she wants to see.

The difference between Dorothea's egotism and Casaubon's is an important one. Dorothea's wants, innocently, to see good; Casaubon's is selfish, utterly unconcerned with the good in any form. Sir James explains to Dorothea his plans for reforming his property's disposition, and "setting a good pattern among his tenants" (8). Brooke objects to Sir James's waste of his money on his tenants, and Dorothea responds, hotly, "Surely . . . it is better to spend money in finding out how men can make the most of the land which supports them all, than in keeping dogs and horses only to gallop over it." She concludes on a moral note: "It is not a sin to make yourself poor in performing experiments for the good of all" (9).

Mr. Brooke answers her typically: "Young ladies don't under-stand political economy, you know. . . . The fact is, human reason may carry you a little too far—over the hedge, in fact." Brooke is "in favour of a little theory," and concedes that "we must have Thought"—but he only wants a "little" thought, because thought is dangerous. Later, trying to agree with Dorothea in her appreciation of thoughtfulness, Brooke says, "I had it myself—that love of knowledge, and going into everything—A little too much—it took me too far" (29). However silly Dorothea may be at times—and she is not in the least silly when she stands up for Sir James's plans for his tenants—Brooke is categor-ically wrong, for George Eliot: Dorothea's thinking is a good thing, and her idealism is the best thing in the novel.

Dorothea's plan for building new cottages is a good thing. Sir James knows this, and appreciates it: she has "the best notion in the world of a plan for cottages" (19). He would like to "carry out that plan" of hers, even though he knows that "Labourers can never pay back rent to make it answer." Still, he says, "it is worth doing" (19).

But in chapter 2 Dorothea ignores Sir James even though he agrees with her. She has her eyes on Casaubon, whom she regards as "the most interesting man she had ever seen" (9). At this point in the novel we have not seen Casaubon yet; we have but Celia's view of him as so "very ugly" (11) to go on. We have, however, heard his conver-sation with Brooke, and can easily concur with Sir James's character-ization of him as "a dried bookworm" (13). Dorothea is correct in rejecting Celia's judgment of Casaubon—"you . . . look upon human beings as if they were merely animals with a toilette, and never see the soul in a great man's face" (11)—but she is wrong in seeing either soul in Casaubon's face or him as a great man. Dorothea's judgment fails her, partly because of her youth and inexperience, partly because of her willfulness and overconfidence. In her vanity, then, she rejects Sir James's kindnesses and good intentions.

Neither George Eliot nor her readers want Dorothea to marry Sir James. That would not be good judgment either. Though Sir James likes Dorothea's "cleverness," he, too, thinks that "mind" is masculine, and that Dorothea should learn to ride well: "Every lady," he says, "ought to be a perfect horsewoman, that she may accompany her husband" (12). When Dorothea rejects this notion—"I shall never correspond to your pattern of a lady"—George Eliot laughs at Sir James and his "man's mind" by giving Dorothea "the air of a handsome boy" (12).

Chapters 3 and 4 are taken up with Dorothea's plans, and the play between Sir James and Casaubon. George Eliot uses Dorothea's plans to introduce the theme of her ambition to "do something," her desire "to make her life greatly effective" (17). When she first asks herself "What could she do, what ought she to do?" (17) perhaps we don't hear what George Eliot has told us about Sir James in chapter 2: that he wanted a wife to whom he could say "What shall we do?" (12). Dorothea isn't thinking of Sir James, either, or hearing him. She is busy dreaming—imagining—her future with Casaubon: "There would be nothing trivial about our lives," she thinks. With Casaubon she will "lead a grand life here—now—in England." In anticipation of such a future, and of knowing "what to do," she determines to "draw plenty of plans while I have time" (18).

Following this brief ecstatic daydream of Dorothea's, Sir James comes to talk to her about what he "wish[es] to do"—which is to use Dorothea's "plan" for building new cottages on his estate (19). Sir James wants to do what is "worth doing." Though Dorothea has no interest in fitting herself to Sir James's "pattern of a lady" (12), she would be very happy to "set the pattern" (20) as to something so worthwhile as cottages for the poor.

Dorothea's plans are very important for the novel. They are literally important, as they represent Dorothea's attempt to do something, to change things that need changing in this world. They are also symbolically important because they represent the idea of change, of reform, of larger sympathies and a larger idea of human life. But plans are not accomplishments, and after her daydreams about living "a grand life" and her conversation with Sir James about her plans, Dorothea quickly discovers that "Mr. Casaubon did not care about building cottages" (21).

It takes a long while in *Middlemarch* for the subject of the Great Reform Bill of 1832 to come up. The novel begins in 1829, and there is constant talk of reform in the novel; Dorothea's plans for cottages are as important to that theme as Lydgate's plans to reform the practice of medicine or Will's activism on behalf of the cause for political reform. Indeed, when we compare these three would-be reformers we realize that Dorothea is the most serious—and the true idealist among them.

Lydgate's ambitions—"to do good small work for Middlemarch, and great work for the world" (102)—are linked with his sense that "his profession . . . wanted reform" (99). But by the time George Eliot tells us about him as a reform-minded professional, we have already met him with Dorothea at Mr. Brooke's. Although he and Dorothea have an "animated conversation"—which Dorothea could never have with Casaubon—and Lydgate finds "her interest in matters socially useful" a relief from the tedium of the party, he judges her as "a little too earnest" and complains to himself that "It is troublesome to talk to such women" (63).

We meet Will but briefly in Book 1 and learn only two things about him: that he refuses conventional life as much as he can, and that he, too, objects to Dorothea's seriousness—she is "unpleasant," and there is "too much cleverness" in her (53). Our sense of Will—here and elsewhere throughout the novel—is that he is more a "dilettantish" (132) rebel than a reformer.

Dorothea, however, is in earnest. And what is most significant about her earnestness, for George Eliot, is the "ardour" (xiii) with which she pursues her ideal, and the "spiritual grandeur" of that ideal itself. Though she may be, finally, the "foundress of nothing" (xiv)—

though she may have found for herself "no epic life" (xiv)—Dorothea is one of the most important people any of us will ever meet. She is so important for the wonderfully simple reason that she is determined to lead a full, rich life in and for a world larger than mere self.

And you and I—what are our determinations? Are we in earnest about anything? Dorothea is a young woman "struggling towards an ideal life" (28). Can we say as much for ourselves? We, perhaps, find it socially awkward or politically difficult to take either ourselves or life seriously. Dorothea, however, is absolutely serious. And though she makes mistakes, they are the result of her inexperience and blindness—vanity is a kind of blindness—rather than the fault of her being so serious and determined. Her seriousness and determination, for George Eliot, are good things.

Celia, Dorothea's younger sister, is not a serious person. At Peter Featherstone's funeral, later on, Celia hides "a little behind her husband's elbow" and refuses to watch: "I shall not look any more" (223). She teases Dorothea's interest: "I daresay Dodo likes it; she is fond of melancholy things and ugly people" (223). Dorothea's reply corrects this silliness with a simple assertion of serious purpose: "I am fond of knowing something about the people I live among" (223).

Dorothea's "people" are the reason for her "plans": and her plans are serious. Early on, when Celia calls them her sister's "favorite fad" (23), Dorothea explodes, wonderfully, in response: "How can one *ever* do anything nobly Christian, living among people with such petty thoughts" (23). To be sure, drawing plans for cottages hardly qualifies as a "nobly Christian" act; but the ambition toward such nobility outweighs the exaggeration. "What was life worth," she thinks, still indignant at Celia's remark, "what great faith was possible when the whole effect of one's actions could be withered up into such parched rubbish as that" (23).

Dorothea wants to be useful. She is not satisfied with the small life that satisfies others. She wants "to judge soundly on the social duties of the Christian," and asks Casaubon, "Could I not be preparing myself to be more useful?" (42). "I have known so few ways of making my life good for anything," she says; "I must learn new ways of helping people" (52). Helping other people is a moral ambition. If, as readers, we have no interest in such ambitions—if we prefer self-interest to society—then we are reading what can only seem a silly novel by a silly novelist. George Eliot believes in society and wants art to "enlarge men's sympathies" for each other. Her moral ambition parallels Dorothea's.

Morality is a good word. In our time, however, it is used most often as a pejorative term for anything that stands in the way of what an individual wants to do. Morality means, these days, "the rules"—and the rules are old-fashioned, best broken or changed or abandoned. Morality—what is called, redundantly, "traditional morality"—is out of date, out of fashion, out of favor. We would prefer, each of us, to be rich.

Rich is what the king is—*rex, regis,* the Latin for king, is cognate to our word—and the king is king by himself. Rich is a comparative word all by itself: one is rich by comparison to someone else, which means that we cannot all be rich. And that creates a problem. King, self, rich: those are not social words, social ideas. They are not moral words either.

A world like ours, which believes—popularly—only in self, necessarily resists the claims of morality. By definition morality is social—and we are not social when we claim king and self and rich as values. *Mores* are conventions or values that enable us to live together. To claim king and self and rich as values is to insist on living apart.

We can agree easily enough—even living apart—that murder is wrong, and we will call it immoral: obviously we cannot all live if we kill each other. But the elaboration of other moral values is more difficult. Morality presumes that we want to live together, as a society. How we do that, or plan to do that, determines our morality.

If in my selfishness I say, "To heck with you—I am looking out for me," I may be speaking as a mainstream modern American, but I am also being antisocial, and my antisocial attitude is undermining the moral values that make it possible for us to live together as Americans. No matter what the economists say in defense of self-interest and capitalism, looking out for me is antisocial and thus by definition immoral. I have an obligation—personal and social—to take care of myself, of course. That is simple prudence. But prudence is not what I have in mind when I decide to look out for me—and to heck with you! Prudence does not justify the claim of self over society.

A few years ago, in a seminar called "Something of Value," my students and I were arguing about Prospero in Shakespeare's *Tempest*. We could just as well have been talking about Dorothea's situation in *Middlemarch*. "You can't govern other people," one student said, "unless you take care of yourself first." A classmate jumped in, and revised that opinion: "You can't take care of other people," she said, "unless you govern yourself first." In an ideal life, we would all be busy taking care of other people, thinking of each other as friends—thinking of each other *as* each other. "What do we live for," Dorothea says, toward the end of the novel, "if it is not to make life less difficult to each other?" (506). To "live for" such a purpose hardly seems heroic, or grand—but for George Eliot it is the "ideal life," toward which Dorothea has been "struggling" throughout the novel.

Along the way Dorothea makes mistakes, certainly, in the passion of her youth; but they are not immoral mistakes. Marrying Edward Casaubon is a mistake, and a costly one. He is a "bladder for dried peas" (38) to Mrs. Cadwallader; his blood is "all semicolons and parentheses" (47). She calls him a "death's head skinned over"; Sir James thinks of him as a "dried bookworm" (13). But Dorothea sees none of this. She is too busy looking for greatness in others and for a chance at generous greatness—heroism—in her own life to be able to see him clearly.

Dorothea has been dreaming of marrying a great man: the venerable Hooker, to save him from his shrewish wife; or Milton, in his blindness; or Locke, or Pascal. She dreams thus not because she is some pitiful "Victorian" woman—let's avoid that dumb stereotype—but because she admires greatness. As of yet she has no understanding of how to be great herself. This is not because she is a woman, but because she is young, and secluded at her uncle's on the outskirts of a small provincial town. "My notion of usefulness," she says, "must be narrow. I must learn new ways of helping people" (52).

George Eliot builds the dramatic tension of the novel from this ambition of Dorothea's and her difficulty in realizing it. Dorothea never becomes a great woman in any public sense, through achievement; she is, as the Prelude forewarns us, "foundress of nothing" (xiv). Her life is radiant, however, for George Eliot: "the effect of her being on those around her was incalculably diffusive"—and "the growing good of the world," she says, comes from such a radiant moral life.

"If Art does not enlarge men's sympathies," George Eliot says, "it does nothing morally." The same can surely be said of life.

· 5 ·

SEEING

It is difficult—or should be—not to sympathize with Dorothea. She wants so much to do good in the world that this yearning burns through to illuminate both her life and the world—even when she makes mistakes.

Dorothea loves Casaubon, or rather she thinks she does. When she sees him, George Eliot says, "the radiance of her transfigured girl-hood" falls on him as "the first object which came within its level" (28). Casaubon's proposal of marriage—"a subject," he writes, "than which I have none more at heart"—is a millstone of pedantry. He writes not of falling in love, but of experiencing "such activity of the affections as even the preoccupations of a work too special to be ab-dicated could not uninterruptedly dissimulate"(27). Several hundred more abstract and sterile words, arranged in convoluted syntax, and he has given Dorothea an "accurate statement of [his] feelings" (28). Dorothea cannot read Casaubon's letter the way we read it, of course, and that is her mistake: she reads what she wants to read, blind to the reality of what his letter tells her. Her reply says, simply, "I am very grateful to you for loving me" (29). It is an answer born of her "pas-sion," George Eliot says, for "a fuller life": her "passion was trans-formed through a mind struggling toward an ideal life" (28).

Seeing

Thomas Hardy, a younger contemporary of George Eliot, comments concerning the young heroine of his novel, *Tess of the D'Urbervilles*, that "experience is as to intensity and not as to duration."[28] That idea is relevant to Dorothea's life, if we add as a corollary that intensity is the significant dimension of life. George Eliot never says this directly, but the idea is there, built very carefully through the imagery of the novel. Another of George Eliot's contemporaries, Walter Pater, writes of intensity like Dorothea's as "burn[ing] always with this hard, gem-like flame." To burn so, he claims, "is success in life."[29] Pater's image of a flame is appropriate for this novel: it is the light within Dorothea, her "radiance" that illuminates the world as she strives for intense life.

George Eliot uses images to build ideas, and by using various images in relation to each of several characters she develops and determines our appreciation for Dorothea. Images collect, arrange themselves in patterns, and begin to offer us larger thematic understandings. Casaubon's dark mind, his weak eyes and "caution about [his] eyesight" (9) are played against Dorothea's myopia and Lydgate's use of the microscope—or the "strange light" in his eyes that suggests his use of opium (442, 463). The idea of vision and what it means to see or to see well is as important as the more simple matter of what one sees; though Dorothea is myopic, she wants to see everything, and that is what's important. Celia, Will Ladislaw, Lydgate, and Dorothea are all associated with yokes and harnesses, and the measure of human freedom. Watching how each of these characters works out his or her life in relation to such ideas of restriction and their images, we come to understand better both the character and his or her comparison to Dorothea.

Before turning to a detailed examination of those two sets of images as they run through the novel, let me consider briefly a smaller example of George Eliot's use of a particular kind of imagery in reference to several characters in order to create and control meaning. Early in the novel, Sir James is made to examine himself in relation to Dorothea, whose talents he so greatly admires: "He was made of excellent human dough, and had the rare merit of knowing that his talents, even if let loose, would not set the smallest stream in the country on fire" (12). Several paragraphs later, at the beginning of chapter 3, Dorothea sits admiring Casaubon. She is "looking into the ungauged reservoir of Mr. Casaubon's mind," George Eliot says; but what she sees there "in vague labyrinthian extension," is "every quality she brought herself" (14). In awe of Casaubon, Dorothea thinks, "his feelings . . . his whole experience—what a lake compared with my little pool" (15).

For Casaubon, awe and admiration are foreign feelings—not so much because he is a proud and vain man, but because he is a selfish and self-centered man. He thinks only of himself and his comforts. He tells Dorothea in his letter that he seeks a wife "to supply aid in graver labours and to cast a charm over vacant hours" (27). As their courtship progresses, he finds it a "hinderance" to his "great work—the Key to All Mythologies" (41). Casaubon has no vitality. What he feels for Dorothea—wanting "to adorn his life with the graces of female companionship, to irradiate the gloom" of his "fatigue," to "secure . . . the solace of female tendance for his declining years" (41)—is not love, but petty self-interest. To describe this pettiness, George Eliot returns to her water image: "he determined to abandon himself to the stream of feeling, and perhaps was surprised to find what an exceedingly shallow rill it was" (41). "Sprinkling," she says, "was the utmost approach to a plunge which his stream would afford him" (42).

The great work of the artist, Pater wrote, is "the transmutation of ideas into images."[30] For George Eliot, the insistently serious and intellectual artist, that is constantly the work at hand. In 1866 she wrote in response to a proposal that she write a philosophically propagandistic novel, "I think aesthetic teaching is the highest of all teaching because it deals with life in its highest complexity. But if it ceases to be purely aesthetic—if it lapses anywhere from the picture to the diagram—it becomes the most offensive of all teaching."[31] Having said this, she rejected the proposal.

Imagery appeals to our senses—specifically to our sense of sight— and expects to excite feeling as well as thought. *Middlemarch* is full of images directly concerned with sight, ranging from comments about lenses and eyesight to discussions of paintings. And related to this imagery is the "radiance" that is Dorothea's from the beginning and is recalled at the end of the novel in the assertion that "the effect of her being on those around her was incalculably diffusive" (578).

George Eliot uses optical imagery in *Middlemarch* to carry the theme of discovery. Just as on the one hand Dorothea plans to do good things for the world—and Lydgate plans to do "great things" for it (102)—so on the other hand George Eliot shows us how difficult it is to discover the world, to know what goodness is, and to accomplish the good in one's life.

Toward the end of chapter 3, Dorothea tells Sir James, "I am rather short-sighted" (19). A few pages later, in chapter 4, Celia chides her sister, concerning Sir James's love for her: "You always see what nobody else sees . . . yet you never see what is quite plain" (23). When Mrs. Cadwallader grills Celia about Dorothea and Casaubon, Celia tries to defend her sister by arguing that "Dodo is very strict. She thinks so much about everything. . . . [but] she does not see things" (36). There is indeed a great deal that Dorothea does not see. What she must learn, as she grows up, is vision—in both senses of the word. She has to learn insight, too—and how not to make mistakes. Dorothea presumes to see a "great soul in [Casaubon's] face" (11); Celia, though not so noble nor so grand as her sister, sees Casaubon much more clearly. And when Celia complains that Dorothea "always sees what nobody else sees," but "never see[s] what is quite plain," we must agree with her criticism. "Miss Brooke was certainly very naive with all her alleged cleverness," George Eliot says; "Celia, whose mind had never been thought too powerful, saw the emptiness of other people's pretensions much more readily" (42).

It may seem odd that so spiritual a young woman as Dorothea would not understand art, but she does not; and this failing tells us, as much as anything in the novel, the limitations of her understanding of the world, of her vision, of her ability to see. Dorothea "understands" what Casaubon calls "the grander forms of music" (43), and she says that she "enjoy[s]" it: "When we were coming home from Lausanne my uncle took us to hear the great organ at Freiberg, and it made me sob" (43). But paintings—paintings of the kind that the narrator, defending Dorothea's bias with her own, calls "severe classical nudities and smirking Renaissance-Correggiosities"—have no appeal for her. They are "painfully inexplicable . . . she had never been taught how she could bring them into any sort of relevance with her life" (49). She tells her uncle, "I never see the beauty of these pictures which you say are so much praised. They are a language I do not understand" (53).

Talking about Dorothea and art brings us necessarily to Will Ladislaw. He and Dorothea have an important discussion of art and its value in Book 2. The conversation about art between Dorothea and Brooke takes place, in fact, on the occasion of Will's introduction. He is sketching, at Lowick, when Dorothea, Casaubon, Celia, and Brooke come upon him. After they leave Will laughs at Casaubon and Brooke, but not at Dorothea. Though he disagrees with her, she is not a fool—like the others are fools. Without intending to do so, she challenges Will's ideas about art and its human or cultural value.

Casaubon describes Will as a young man "without any special object" in life "save the vague purpose of what he calls culture." In response to Casaubon's urging of purposeful exploration and the acquisition of factual knowledge, Will has said that he "should prefer not to know the source of the Nile . . . [so] that there should be some unknown regions preserved as hunting-grounds for the poetic imagination" (54). To Casaubon this attitude is part of Will's "self-indulgent taste"(55).

Though Dorothea does not understand art and has a general aversion to waste of any sort, particularly the waste of a life, she does defend Will: "people may really have in them some vocation which is not quite plain to themselves. . . . They may seem idle and weak because they are growing" (55). George Eliot is not very sympathetic to Will; she lets the painter Naumann call him "dilettantish" (132), and later herself refers to his "dilettanteism" (319). But Will's ideas and attitudes serve as an important complement to Dorothea's. Her sense of duty and her desire to grow "wise" (42) by submission to the wisdom of others plays against Will's insistence on independence and his own free growth. Will "call[s] himself Pegasus," Casaubon charges, "and every form of prescribed work 'harness'" (55).

Though Dorothea never asserts her freedom in such a way, her freedom is what *Middlemarch* is about. Dorothea does not claim to be a poet, either—as Will does, in calling himself "Pegasus"—but her imagination is the greatest imagination in the novel. Eventually Will calls her not a poet, but a "poem" (156)—and being a poem is greater, I suspect, than being Saint Theresa or the Blessed Virgin (529) or a Christian Antigone (132). In the end, Dorothea's imagination creates not just poetry or art, but life. In Dorothea, the idea of knowledge usually represented in the imagery of seeing is transformed into the idea of sympathetic understanding that we call feeling. And feeling, then, becomes vision—radiant vision, poetry itself.

Will's refusal of "harness" is the image-reference for another important idea in *Middlemarch*. The theme of restriction is introduced in the final lines of the first chapter. Celia, we are told, "had always worn a yoke" in her relationship with Dorothea; "but is there any yoked creature," the narrator asks, "without its private opinions?" (7). Mr. Brooke uses the image again, talking about marriage: "I never loved anyone well enough to put myself into a noose for them. It *is* a noose, you know" (26). And just after Casaubon has talked about Will as rejecting "harness," the narrator explains Ladislaw's belief that "genius . . . is necessarily intolerant of fetters" (55).

Lydgate, too, determines to avoid restrictions. Talking with Farebrother about "wearing harness," Lydgate says, "I made up my mind some time ago to do as little of it as possible" (120). Lydgate has ambitions—a "plan," like Dorothea's: he wants "to do good small work for Middlemarch, and great work for the world" (102). He intends to "reform" his profession (99–101) in a variety of ways, and is confident of his ability to do so. But Lydgate's confidence is not an unalloyed asset. The first time we see him, at Mr. Brooke's party late in Book 1, he is not a very congenial character. He and Dorothea have "a very animated conversation" about "cottages and hospitals" (62), and he is agreeably surprised by Dorothea's "interest in matters socially useful." But he finds Dorothea "a little too earnest," and concludes his observation with a grossly chauvinistic thought about "troublesome . . . women," whom he considers generally "ignorant" (63). "Miss Brooke," he thinks, does not "look at things from the proper female angle" (64).

Lydgate's ideal of female society is "reclining in a paradise with sweet laughs for bird-notes, and blue eyes for a heaven" (64). As though catering to his desire, George Eliot immediately produces, seemingly for his pleasure, Rosamond Vincy. Rosamond decides to have Lydgate, however, and "harnesses" him with little trouble, despite his intentions of remaining independent of any such attachment.

Lydgate has "abundant kindness [in] his heart," and an earnest "belief that human life might be made better" (105). He is serious about his scientific ambition to do "good work . . . and great work," and when he leaves the Vincy home after a pleasant evening there he thinks not of Rosamond but of work. He delights in his scientific ability, and is convinced of his superiority over the other medical practitioners in the neighborhood. But for all that Lydgate seems to be an excellent scientist whose keen analytical eye is a superb "lens," he is blind to much that goes on around him. His blindness comes from crudeness and callowness, not—like Dorothea's—from innocent would-be idealism. Lydgate is "ardent," like Dorothea; but unlike Dorothea's "ardor," Lydgate's is all selfish (114). As he looks at himself, he thinks, "I should never have been happy in any profession that did not call forth the highest intellectual strain, and keep me in good warm contact with my neighbours. There is nothing like the medical profession for that: one can have the exclusive scientific life that touches the distance and befriend the old fogies in the parish too" (114). The man who thinks of his "neighbours" as "the old fogies in the parish" is hardly an honestly kind-hearted man—nor does he understand those "old fogies" very well. "Middlemarch," George Eliot warns, "counted on swallowing Lydgate and assimilating him very comfortably" (105).

Lydgate's vain self-confidence causes his downfall. He thinks he is in control of his life and can afford to relax, to quit thinking and enjoy himself. Whereas Dorothea's seriousness traps her into marrying Casaubon, Lydgate's assumption that he can have a half-serious life— that he can quit taking his own life seriously on weekends—lets Rosamond trap him. Because Dorothea is serious, she survives her mistake: learns from it, grows through it. Lydgate assumes that his ambitions and ideals are so secure that he can forget them for a time and come back to them when he is ready to. He thinks he is strong enough to afford a bit of diversion, an occasional bit of thoughtlessness. This lack of seriousness destroys him.

Dorothea is introduced at the beginning of *Middlemarch* as a young woman who takes both herself and this world seriously. Her mistakes come from an overconfidence that will not let her examine her ideals and ambitions critically. Certain that she is right, she indulges in righteousness and makes mistakes. But her mistakes are not fatal; her absolute respect for the idea of righteousness—her belief in the idea of a life of principle and principled acts—saves her, even in her marriage to Casaubon.

In Book 2 we are introduced to Lydgate as a young man who thinks he takes himself and his work seriously, but who does so only on a part-time basis. Lydgate lacks any sense of principle; he is a creature of ambitions more than of ideals. His lack of principle—his lack of respect, finally, for his own life—destroys him.

Lydgate is warned by Mrs. Bulstrode about the meaning given in Middlemarch to his attentions to Rosamond. As a result, he "resolve[s]" to give up visiting the Vincy house "except on business" (207), determining to stick to his work and "give up going out in the evening" (206). But eleven days later he abandons this "resolution," visits Rosamond, and "forgetting everything else" becomes engaged. When he leaves her house his "soul [is] not his own, but the woman's to whom he had bound himself" (208).

It is not solely in his marriage to Rosamond that Lydgate learns to "wear the harness" that he has "determined" not to wear (120); Bulstrode comes to own him as well. And Lydgate falls into dependence on Bulstrode in the same, easy, thoughtless, arrogant way that he falls into servitude to Rosamond. Farebrother warns Lydgate about Bulstrode, but he will not listen. When Lydgate discovers that he is expected to vote on the choice of a chaplain for his new fever hospital, he is "vexed" at having to concern himself in such "trivial Middlemarch business" (123). His vexation grows as he begins to feel "the hampering threadlike pressure of small social conditions, and their frustrating complexity" (124). With his "unmixed resolutions of independence," he resents finding himself "in the grasp of petty alternatives" (124). Busy being "vexed," Lydgate doesn't bother to consider how he will cast his ballot. The time comes for voting, and he votes impulsively. He casts his ballot for Mr. Tyke in order to prove his independence: he will not be forced by circumstances to vote for Farebrother in order to demonstrate his freedom from Bulstrode. He is free, he says, to vote for or against Bulstrode's candidate—and he votes for him. He recognizes immediately that he has compromised himself: "If he had been quite free from indirect bias he should have voted for Mr. Farebrother." He is forced to admit to himself that "this petty medium of Middlemarch [has] been too strong for him" (129).

George Eliot works comparatively, and through comparison she leads us toward acts of judgment. We see similar deeds—Farebrother, Fred Vincy, and Lydgate all gamble, for example; Lydgate and Will are both offered money by Bulstrode—and we compare acts and thoughts and manners which, though different, are presented similarly.

Metaphors, the poet Shelley says, are "the before unapprehended relations of things." They "perpetuate . . . apprehension" until we have established for ourselves the meanings of these new relations or the meanings available through them.[32] George Eliot shows us Farebrother earnestly playing whist, and has Lydgate wonder "whether Mr. Farebrother cared about the money he won at cards" (112). Farebrother does care: he supplements his meager income with his small winnings at whist. He also plays billiards for money sometimes at the Green Dragon (123). Later we find out that Fred has been playing billiards and losing; he has run up a debt of "a hundred and sixty pounds" (158). But George Eliot insists that Fred is "not a gambler," that he "had not that specific disease" (162). Still, he gambles again, trying to cover his losses by trading horses—and irresponsibly loses Caleb Garth's money.

Lydgate has witnessed gambling in Paris, "watching it as if it had been a disease" (462). When, under the stress of debts, he finds himself in the Green Dragon and playing a game of billiards "for the sake of passing the time," he starts to gamble on his own play. Under the influence of winning and being "confident" in his game, he soon begins to have "visions . . . of going the next day to Brassing, where there was gambling on a grander scale to be had" (463).

Of course, we compare Lydgate's gambling with Fred's and Farebrother's; to ensure that we do, George Eliot brings them both into the scene. Farebrother's gambling is no sin or crime or disease; among other things, he knows what he is doing, and it is sober work rather than frenzied play. Fred's gambling is stupid and irresponsible; the terms in which he is criticized for it become part of another comparison we will discuss later. But Lydgate's gambling becomes an emblem, in the novel, for the failure of his character. There is something about Lydgate: something wrong with him.

Both Lydgate and Casaubon marry, but we would not think of comparing either them or their marriages were it not that George Eliot sets up such a comparison for us. Both men are scholars, of sorts; but Casaubon is a dull, middle-aged pedant, and Lydgate is a bright and talented young doctor. Both men are self-centered, however—and this flaw shows first and most clearly in their attitude toward women.

I have already discussed Casaubon's notions of marriage: his work is what is important to him, but he also wants to "adorn his life with the graces of female companionship" and "irradiate the gloom"

MIDDLEMARCH

of his life with "the play of female fancy" (41)—an attitude that is an insult to Dorothea in particular and to women in general. Lydgate has no plans to marry when first we meet him; his "ardor" is "absorbed in love of his work" (114). But Rosamond quickly changes his plans. Though he talks to Rosamond "of his hopes as to the highest uses of his life," he thinks of her not as involved in such uses but rather as "a creature who would bring him the sweet furtherance of satisfying affection—beauty—repose—such help as our thoughts get from the summer sky and the flower-fringed meadows" (245). When we read this we should think not only of Lydgate's earlier notion of "reclining in a paradise with sweet laughs for bird-notes and blue eyes for a heaven" (64), but also of Casaubon's condescending attitude toward women. To do so is not to import modern attitudes into *Middlemarch;* rather, it is to read the novel that George Eliot wrote.

Because of his interest in reforming his profession Lydgate can also be compared with Will, the political reformer, and with Dorothea, who would change this world. Lydgate knows what he wants to do: "the broad road . . . was quite ready made" (64). Dorothea, on the other hand, keeps asking what she can do; she has not yet found her "road." Lydgate is a scientist; he uses the microscope—figuratively as well as literally—"to pierce the obscurity of those minute processes which prepare human misery and joy . . . which determine the growth of happy or unhappy consciences (113). But despite his work—despite his profound knowledge and his skill, despite his ambition "to do good small work for Middlemarch, and great work for the world" (102)—Lydgate fails. He asks Farebrother about a former friend of his, another doctor named Trawley who has grand ambitions of his own about changing the world. The answer to the question about Trawley is that he is "practicing at a German bath, and has married a rich patient" (119). Trawley's ambitions and his ideals have failed him. In the end Lydgate joins Trawley, metaphorically. He divides his practice between London and "a Continental bathing-place"; his contribution to science is "a treatise on Gout, a disease which has a good deal of wealth on its side" (575). He devotes himself to providing for the "bird of paradise" who was supposed to entertain him, and dies prematurely, "a failure" who "had not done what he once meant to do" (575).

Lydgate's failure is a failure of character. When we look at all the evidence concerning his character that George Eliot gives us we discover that the self-proclaimed reformer and scientific idealist is in fact a careless materialist, and that his materialism corrupts his life. When we look at Lydgate under George Eliot's microscope we see not just a man married to a materialistic and selfish wife; we also see a materialistic and self-indulgent man who has married a beautiful woman for his own pleasure. When the crisis comes for Lydgate, George Eliot presents it as a material crisis first: he wants money. When the moral or spiritual crisis comes—at the death of Raffles—Lydgate has already mortgaged what principles he has, and can only leave town, morally and spiritually bankrupt.

Lydgate is hardly a sympathetic character; in his weakness he is pitiable, perhaps. He doesn't learn anything. He submits himself to his own failure. That "he regarded himself as a failure," at the end of the novel, scarcely moves us to sympathy: he has chosen "paying patients" over a life of honor and value.

When we first meet Lydgate, he is a "man . . . still in the making." "Character," George Eliot reminds us, "is a process and an unfolding." But then she catalogs Lydgate's faults of character: he is "arrogant," "a little too self-confident and disdainful" (102). She concludes her analysis tellingly: "Lydgate's spots of commonness lay in the complexion of his prejudices. . . that distinction of mind which belonged to his intellectual ardour did not penetrate his feeling and judgment about furniture, or women. . . . He did not mean to think of furniture at present; but whenever he did so [he experienced] the vulgarity of feeling that there would be an incompatibility in his furniture not being of the best" (103).

For all that Will Ladislaw is a dilettante, he does have values and principles, and he is looking for something to do with his whole life. He is not a materialist—though he does live off of Casaubon's allowance. When Bulstrode, to ease his own guilty conscience, offers Will money, Will refuses it. We compare this act, of course, to Lydgate's acceptance of Bulstrode's aid. Lydgate believes—as he did while gambling at the Green Dragon—that money will save him. Will knows better.

When Will and Dorothea finally marry, they must give up money in order to do so. Dorothea has already determined not to let Casaubon's cruel attempt to "harness" her to his failure corrupt her ambition or her life. Will—selflessly—has determined to go away from the woman he loves. Now they are free to marry.

After Dorothea has seen—seen, but misunderstood—Will playing with Rosamond, she goes to Freshitt Hall, determined more than ever to be "ardent in readiness to be [Lydgate's] champion." When she enters the drawing room, Celia cries, "Dodo, how very bright your eyes are! . . . And you don't see anything you look at." Dorothea's response is that she has seen "all the troubles of all people on the face of the earth" (535). What she has seen is her own trouble—if trouble it be. When she is alone she moans, thinking of Will, "Oh, I did love him!" (542).

What follows is Dorothea's dark night of loneliness and spiritual pain. When morning comes, she resolves—in spite of her hurt—to be "more helpful"; resorting to her old formula, she asks herself "What should I do—how should I act, this very day, if I could clutch my own pain, and compel it to silence, and think of those three?" (544). George Eliot answers Dorothea's noble question by showing her a vision. Her vision is of the "road" that Lydgate thought was "ready made" before him (64). The morning's "light" pierces into Dorothea's room, and she looks out on "the bit of road" outside her window: "On the road there was a man with a bundle on his back and a woman carrying her baby; in the field she could see figures moving—perhaps the shepherd with his dog. Far off in the bending sky was the pearly light; and she felt the largeness of the world and the manifold wakings of men to labour and endurance" (544). Dorothea dresses herself, then, and sets off "toward Middlemarch." Her ambition now is "to see and save Rosamond" (545).

Seeing

In her pain Dorothea learns to "see." She tells Will, "If we had lost our own chief good, other people's good would remain, and that is worth trying for. . . . I seemed to see that more clearly than ever" (558). That Dorothea sees so clearly now results from her own goodness, not from her application to Lydgate's microscope.

In 1860 George Eliot wrote, "The highest 'calling and election' is to *do without opium* and live through all out pain with conscious, clear-eyed endurance."[33] Had the date been right, she could have been talking about Dorothea and Lydgate. Lydgate closes his eyes to things, hides from pain, uses opium to distract himself or numb himself into endurance. Dorothea—for all her myopia—wants always to see things, and learns to see them "clearly." The vision which George Eliot gives her—of the road, the sky full of "pearly light"—is a work of art. Dorothea creates it, by knowing how to look out of her own soul at this large world of "labour and endurance" (544). There is no mistake, now, in what or how she sees.

• 6 •

FEELING AND KNOWLEDGE

George Eliot is a formidable woman. Perhaps no young man of Lydgate's age should be forced to submit himself to her for judgment. She
pretends, of course, not to judge him: his character, she tells the
reader, is still in the making, "a process and an unfolding" (102). But
she does judge him, calling him arrogant and self-centered, careless
and overconfident: an egotist, in short. In his actions he proves her
right.

It is not that George Eliot manipulates Lydgate, or for that matter
other characters in *Middlemarch*. Her method, most of the time, is a
humanistically didactic one that examines a character's flaws and fa-
vors in such a way as to make that examination carry her unspoken
authorial judgment. George Eliot's generalizations about characters in
Middlemarch are usually condescending, not just because she doesn't
particularly like those about whom she makes generalizations but because—like the god who foreknows but does not predestine—they can
only prove, in their lives, her judgment of them.

George Eliot is particularly hard on Lydgate because he could
easily fool us. Like Dorothea, he has ambitions to "do something"

worthwhile. She does not know yet "what to do"; he plans to "do good small work for Middlemarch, and great work for the world" (102). Like Dorothea, he wants to reform things. Like her, he is unconventional. It would be wonderful, we think—or might think—if he and Dorothea could marry.

But what would be the result of such a marriage? Dorothea would do her plans for cottages, and Lydgate would "do good work" in his hospital and maybe even more. But neither of them would be tested in any serious way. Married to a rich woman, Lydgate would not have to worry about money. The flaws in his character might never show themselves. Married to a doctor with grand ambitions for himself, Dorothea would never have to examine her ideals and might grow old still planning cottages and submitting her life to someone else's. If Lydgate and Dorothea married, Dorothea would very likely lose her life to his success. Many women with great potential for illuminating this world have suffered such a fate in the service of husbands much less enlightened, and much less interested in the light. I do not think George Eliot could let Dorothea fail this way: George Eliot's moral argument requires more of her heroine—and our world needs her light.

The first clue we have to the importance of Will Ladislaw for the novel comes in Dorothea's defense of him: "people may really have in them some vocation which is not quite plain to themselves. . . . They may seem idle and weak because they are growing" (55). Lydgate is a "man . . . still in the making" (102) for George Eliot—but he thinks of himself as already made, and is confident of his future. All that Will knows yet is that he cannot afford to waste his life.

A wasted life is a terrible thing. When Mary Garth fights with Fred Vincy it is over "doing something" versus being "an idle frivolous creature." "How can you bear to be so contemptible," she says, chiding and challenging him, "when others are working and striving, and there are so many things to be done—how can you bear to be fit for nothing in the world that is useful?" (176). Lydgate does not need to ask himself such a question; he knows that he is useful, professionally, and he feels both "a triumphant delight in his studies and something like pity for those less lucky who were not of his profession" (113). Knowing that he is useful, Lydgate becomes self-satisfied—and his usefulness begins to dissipate. Dorothea burns with Mary's question, however, and so does Will. They ask it of themselves.

Midway through Book 2, George Eliot turns her attention from Lydgate in Middlemarch to Dorothea in Rome. Lydgate has been to a party at the Vincy's now, and though it is "certainly not [an] erudite household" he can "half-understand" Farebrother's contentment visiting there: "the good humour, the good looks of elder and younger, and the promise of passing the time without any labour of intelligence might make the house beguiling to people who had no particular use for their odd hours" (111). For himself, "Lydgate did not mean to pay many . . . visits himself. They were a wretched waste of the evenings" (111). The next thing Lydgate does, however, is tell Rosamond that he would like to "dance" with her, and in effect promises to attend at her father's house the next time they "have dancing" (112). And then there's that "trivial Middlemarch business" (123)—of the chaplaincy at the hospital—which interferes with his important work.

When we get to Rome, in chapter 19, the narrative voice introduces this new world in such a way as to suggest the expansion of possibilities, not their contraction. The previous chapters have been designed "to make . . . Lydgate better known to any one interested in him than he could possibly be even to those who had seen the most of him since his arrival in Middlemarch" (96). To do this, George Eliot says, she has "concentrated all the light [she] can" on "unravelling certain human lots, and seeing how they were woven and interwoven"; she has focused on "this particular web," and not on "that tempting range of relevancies called the universe" (96). By the end of chapter 18, Lydgate feels "the hampering threadlike pressure of small social conditions, and their frustrating complexity" (124) and admits that "this petty medium of Middlemarch ha[s] been too strong for him" (129). He is caught in the "web," despite all his ambitions toward the "universe"—or "great good for the world" (102).

Feeling and Knowledge

In Rome—in the "universe" of "relevancies" beyond Middle-march—things are different. It is not that Rome is particularly modern or open or free; rather, despite the ignorance of "the world in general" (130), Rome holds possibilities for those whose minds are open. Whereas Lydgate's story is one of closing opportunities and diminishing ambitions, Dorothea's is one of openness and growth. Her growth begins in Rome and with the reintroduction of Will, who is already there.

George Eliot's focus in talking about Lydgate is often science; here, in talking about Dorothea, it is art, the kind of moral art that will "enlarge men's sympathies." When Dorothea arrives in Rome, "Romanticism," which George Eliot connects with "love and knowledge," is "fermenting" there as a "vigorous enthusiasm" (130). One of the enthusiasts is Will—and he talks to Dorothea throughout her time there. Their talks are serious arguments about serious things, not flirtations to the accompaniment of light music and the prospects of dancing.

In the first half of Book 2 George Eliot tells us much about Lydgate's medical education and how much he knows; in the second half, we come eventually to talk about knowledge itself, and what it is worth. In the first half of the book we get Farebrother's collection of "specimen," which—because it has no grand significance—bores Lydgate; in the second half we get poor Casaubon's collection of scholarly minutiae, scorned and laughed at by Will. In the first half we are introduced to that lovely little woman Henrietta Noble, who is a sugar-thief philanthropist; in the second we get Dorothea's "active sympathy" (141) and the argument about doing good. The world of Middlemarch, in the first half of Book 2, is chattering noisily, sometimes to Lydgate's dismay though at other times to his distracted amusement. In Rome, we are threatened by "that roar which lies on the other side of silence" (135).

Our first look at Rome is over the shoulders of Will and his German artist friend Adolf Naumann; what we see is Dorothea in a museum. She is posed, thoughtfully, in juxtaposition with the sculpture of Ariadne in the Vatican galleries. Naumann sees her as a painting:

she is "the most perfect young Madonna," "a sort of Christian Antigone." She symbolizes, for him, "sensuous force controlled by spiritual
passion" (132).

We have to stop here, briefly, to identify historically what Naumann represents in the novel. *Middlemarch* takes place, George Eliot
says, at the time when "Romanticism . . . was fermenting still as a
distinguishable vigorous enthusiasm in certain long-haired German
artists in Rome" (130). Ladislaw's sketching—and his thinking—lead
him to an association with one of those artists. Naumann may have
been George Eliot's version of the founder of the German Nazarene
school, Johann Friedrich Overbeck (1789–1869), who worked in
Rome after 1810.[34] Certainly Naumann is a representative of that
school; his characterization of Dorothea as "antique form animated
by Christian sentiment—a sort of Christian Antigone—sensuous
form controlled by spiritual passion" (133) is a perfect Nazarene
description.

The Nazarenes sought to revivify art by recharging symbolism
with emotion, particularly with spiritual or religious emotion. They
rejected simple classicism as abstractly intellectual. They were themselves intellectuals—but they insisted that ideas must excite feelings.
If Naumann wanted to paint Antigone he would want a modern
young woman like Dorothea, whose passion he immediately recognizes, for his model. When he asks Casaubon to be his model for Saint
Thomas Aquinas, he explains that he sees in Casaubon's face "the
idealistic in the real" (149)—which is precisely what a Nazarene
wants.

By 1850 the Nazarenes had important disciples in England
known as the Pre-Raphaelites, led in literature and in art by young
Dante Gabriel Rossetti. In 1870, just as she was starting to work on
Middlemarch, George Eliot went to see some of Rossetti's paintings;
four months later he sent her a copy of his new book, *Poems.*[35] It is
more than likely that Rossetti in some sense served her as the model
for Will.

As Will argues with Naumann, the Nazarene accuses Will of

Dante Gabriel Rossetti: Self-portrait, age 18.
Courtesy of National Portrait Gallery, London.

being "dilettantish and amateurish." Will admits the charge: "I am amateurish," he says (132). But he loves the beautiful, and Naumann's ideas about "symbolic" art do not satisfy him: "I do *not* think that all the universe is straining toward the obscure significance of your pictures" (132). Will goes on to argue for the superiority of literature to the plastic arts: "Language is a finer medium. . . . Language gives a fuller image, which is all the better for being vague" (133).

The important point here is not the assertion that language is better or more expressive than paint, or even that suggestive vagueness is better than detailed, determinate precision. The point is that we are in the middle of an argument about the value of art. Will's notion of vagueness and suggestion is important, both for the Nazarenes and Pre-Raphaelites and for George Eliot; its corollary—that "the true seeing is within" (133) has special significance, here as well as later in the novel.

Ladislaw's role in *Middlemarch* is in part established by means of his association with Pre-Raphaelitism: it gives him a set of basic values from which to develop his personal identity. The historical association gives authority—but not necessarily approval—to his character and his way of life. It does not prohibit George Eliot from criticizing him for being a dilettante, though even in that criticism she seems to recognize the measure of his spiritual potential. When he gives up "poetic metres" and "medievalism"—which is to say the Pre-Raphaelite affectation—in exchange for the chance of "sympathising warmly with liberty and progress in general" (318), George Eliot comments that "Our sense of duty must often wait for some work which shall take the place of dilettanteism and make us feel that the quality of our action is not a matter of indifference" (318–19). She is almost quoting Dorothea's earlier defense of him: "people may really have some vocation in them which is not quite plain to themselves. They may seem idle and weak because they are growing" (55).

Of course, Will has never been a petty creature, merely a dilettante. His moral point of view is a serious one. His religion, he says, is "To love what is good and beautiful when I see it" (271). True, by comparison with Dorothea's ambition, to *do* good for other people, Will's ambition sounds effetely aesthetic, "dilettantish." And adumbrating the decadents of the 1890s, he insists to Dorothea, "I don't feel bound, as you do, to submit to what I don't like" (271). Still, his point of view is important for the novel, and important for Dorothea to understand.

Will is critical of Naumann's symbolic understanding of Dorothea, though we perhaps should not be. When Naumann describes her as "sensuous force controlled by spiritual passion" he has seen her complexity clearly. Dorothea is indeed a passionate woman—as we shall see in the next chapter; and her passion is certainly "spiritual." She is also sensuously beautiful, with or without emeralds; and she is so very alive that it is not at all an exaggeration to call her energy of being something like a "force." The problem with Naumann's description is that we don't usually think of "passion" as a control.

When we see Dorothea in the chapter that follows this scene in the Vatican museum, she is crying. She has just returned from the Vatican and is sitting "alone" in the "inner room" of her apartment (133). We see inside her mind and find there her grief: "the true seeing is within." She has "no distinctly shapen grievance"; her sense of the wrong done her—by Casaubon—is vague and confused, but none the less real for being so. She examines her pain: "in the midst of her confused thought and passion, the mental act that was struggling forth into cleverness was a self-accusing cry that . . . the fault [was] her own spiritual poverty" (133).

She is wrong, of course, in her self-accusation. But she does have something to learn about how to do good things for others. The cause of her sorrow is Casaubon's cruel rejection of her suggestion that he begin to publish—with her help—his great work. She misjudges him in this matter, just as she has misjudged him in everything else. She is "blind" to his "terror": in her ardent desire to help him, she threatens and accuses him. For all of her generosity, Dorothea has "not yet listened patiently to his heart-beats, but only felt that her own was beating violently" (139).

Dorothea's mistake is not in wanting to help Casaubon, but in failing to understand his vanity and vulnerability. Dorothea has not yet achieved or acquired that "keen vision and feeling" that will let her understand Casaubon. To have "a keen vision and feeling of all ordinary human life," George Eliot says, "would be like hearing the grass grow and the squirrel's heart beat, and we should die of that roar which lies on the other side of silence." But most of us needn't worry: even "the quickest of us walk about well wadded with stupidity" (135).

Dorothea, however, is "crying," alone in her "inner room"—and she is beginning to undo and discard some of that wadding. She knows that something is wrong. She has only "general words" so far for what it is; but she knows—feels—that her marriage is already failing. Teasing, George Eliot reminds us that such a sense is not so very unusual: "In this way, the early months of marriage often are times of critical tumult—whether that of a shrimp-pool or of deeper waters—which afterwards subsides into cheerful peace" (135). Most of us get over wanting very much from life, she says—but Dorothea doesn't.

Compared to Casaubon, Dorothea has too great a "capacity of thought and feeling," and "What was fresh to her mind was worn out to his" (136). Unlike hers, his mind is "a sort of dried preparation, a lifeless embalmment of knowledge" (137). Full of "thought and feeling," Dorothea pushes, demanding life. Casaubon's is "a mind weighted with unpublished matter" (138), and Dorothea suggests to him that, with her help, he begin to unload that weight and become what she would be, "useful": "All those rows of volumes—will you not now do what you used to speak of?—will you not make up your mind . . . and begin to write the book which will make your vast knowledge useful to the world?" (139). To be "useful" herself, she offers to assist him: "I can be of no other use," she says, pathetically.

But Dorothea's request is a mistake. In her desire to make something worthwhile of her life, she fails to see that Casaubon cannot make such of his. He has built a huge card-house of expectation, of research—but that is all he has. There is no "Key to All Mythologies"—or if there is, he certainly does not have it and never will. As we find out from Ladislaw, Casaubon does not know German and is thus cut off from the most important work done on his subject; he is "not an Orientalist" either (144, 154).

Dorothea's suggestion threatens Casaubon. Her anxious desire to be useful—to make sense of her own life—intrudes upon his thin security. He rejects her proposal angrily: "My love . . . you may rely on me for knowing the times and seasons adapted to the different stages of [my] work" (139). He insults her, referring to the "facile conjectures of ignorant onlookers." His work is "beyond their reach," he claims haughtily, and he resents the intrusion of "superficial" judgment (140). Her response is indignant: though her "judgment was a very superficial one," she only wanted "to be of some good" to him (140).

As a result of this confrontation, Dorothea begins to see her future more clearly. She and Casaubon drive in silence to the Vatican, where he leaves her in the museum. Ignoring the works of art among which she stands, Dorothea sees "inwardly . . . the light of years to come in her own home and over the English fields and elms and hedge-bordered highroads" (141).

It is while Dorothea stands there, "inwardly seeing," that Naumann and Will come upon her. Will concludes that earlier chapter talking about precisely the kind of seeing that Dorothea is doing here: "the true seeing," he says, "is within" (133). Will knows what Dorothea feels.

If Dorothea were any lesser creature she would perhaps break down altogether at this point. But she does not. Her strength of character keeps her tears from overcoming her: "In Dorothea's mind there was a current into which all thought and feeling were apt sooner or later to flow—the reaching forward of the whole consciousness towards the fullest truth, the least partial good" (141). As of yet Dorothea does not know what her alternative to frustration and pain can be; "thought and feeling" are as yet still vague. But "there was something," she concludes, "better than anger and despondency" (141). The alternative that she chooses is to be, in general terms, "alive to everything that gave her an opportunity for active sympathy" (141). In response to this determination on Dorothea's part, George Eliot produces Will.

Dorothea has had an "animated conversation" with Lydgate earlier, about "cottages and hospitals" (62), at the end of which Lydgate decided that she was "too earnest"—and really "too ignorant to understand" such things (63). Ladislaw and Dorothea now engage in an animated conversation for the next two chapters, and Will begins by telling Dorothea that he suspects her "of knowing so much" (143). They are in earnest as they talk—and they talk about things altogether beyond Lydgate's understanding or interest. To Lydgate, "women . . . too ignorant to understand the merits of any question . . . usually fall back on their moral sense to settle things" (63). Dorothea and Will talk seriously about morality—and their conversation on the subject is probably the most important conversation in the whole novel.

Back in the first part of Book 2 we watched Middlemarch respectability at work, in parties at the Vincys' and in Lydgate's professional alliances and misalliances. We saw Lydgate getting involved in the web of respectability, and about to get married. In the second half of the book we are with Dorothea, on her honeymoon tour to Rome. She is married—and she is being quite seriously unrespectable, in a sense, in her relationship with Will. I do not mean that there is anything sexual or socially compromising about it, and it is not—again—that Victorians were prudes. By calling Dorothea "unrespectable" in her conduct I mean that she is not settling down properly into boredom—into what George Eliot called, a few pages back "cheerful peace" (135). Dorothea is engaged in a vital, passionate argument with Will. They are arguing about life.

These two chapters—21 and 22—weave back and forth, braiding the two strands of Casaubon's work and Dorothea's and Will's conversation about art. Will thinks of Casaubon as a "Bat of erudition," a "dried-up pedant," an "elaborator of small explanations" (142). He curses Casaubon, silently, for deserting Dorothea and justifies his talk with Dorothea as his rescue of his lovely cousin.

Feeling and Knowledge

Will begins by complimenting Dorothea on "knowing so much," but she insists that her criticism of his sketching, at Lowick, was "really . . . ignorance," not knowledge (143). She explains: "There are comparatively few paintings that I can enjoy. . . . It is painful to be told that anything is very fine and not be able to feel that it is fine—something like being blind when people talk of the sky" (143). Then she turns the subject, in her usual way, toward real doing in the real world. Art seems to her not enough, not close enough to life: "in Rome is seems as if there were so many things which are more wanted in the world than pictures" (143). When Dorothea turns their attention from art to "things more wanted than pictures," she is not simply disparaging art; rather, she now urges Will—if he wants to be an artist—to make art "do," somehow, what needs to be done. Awkwardly, talk of usefulness brings them to Casaubon, and Will explains the flaw in Casaubon's education. Dorothea's response is typical Dorothea: "How I wish I had learned German when I was at Lausanne [in school]. . . . But now I can be of no use" (145).

As George Eliot concludes this chapter, she presents the argument that Dorothea's selflessness—her desire to "be of . . . use"—is not enough, or good enough, to build a life on. "We are all of us born in moral stupidity," she says, "taking the world as an udder to feed our supreme selves." Dorothea began very early in life "to emerge from that stupidity" (146) and care for others. But she has not yet learned to make of that care for others the kind of sympathetic understanding that George Eliot requires of us. Dorothea has not yet learned that Casaubon, for example, has "an equivalent center of self" of his own; and however much we may dislike that center, criticize it for its vanity, or deplore its imposition on Dorothea, George Eliot insists that her heroine must learn to sympathize with it.

The language she uses for this is telling. She asks Dorothea "to conceive with that distinctness which is no longer reflection but feeling—an idea wrought back to the directness of sense" (146). Dorothea already knows how to understand with "thought and feeling" (141) for herself, and how to make of the act of self-understanding

MIDDLEMARCH

something "which is no longer reflection but feeling" (146). She must learn now how to do that for others.

At the end of chapter 20, the "current" of "thought and feeling" in Dorothea has dried her tears, and she is confident that there is "clearly something better than anger and despondency" (141). At the end of chapter 21, she is on the verge of learning what that "something better" is: she has "felt the waking of a presentiment that there might be a sad consciousness in [Casaubon's] life which made as great a need on his side as on her own" (146). What she needs to get beyond this "presentiment" is further development of that way of seeing life which George Eliot calls "sympathy." She comes to that in chapter 22, as she talks again with Will, about art.

"I fear you are a heretic about art," Will remarks: "I should have expected you to be very sensitive to the beautiful everywhere." Dorothea answers: "I suppose I am dull about many things. . . . I should like to make life beautiful—I mean everybody's life." She is disturbed by the "expense of art," and complains that art "seems somehow to lie outside of life" and that "most people are shut out from it" (152). Will objects: "I call that the fanaticism of sympathy" (152). "The best piety is to enjoy—when you can. You are doing the most then to save the earth's character as an agreeably planet. And enjoyment radiates" (153).

In the end of the novel these two perspectives—these two seemingly uncongenial, contradictory idealisms—will have to be resolved, united. The moral ideal to which Dorothea is devoted and the aesthetic ideal—"the best piety is to enjoy"—by which Will wants to live will be reconciled by the necessary compromise which fulfills both, without a surrender of principle on either side. Ladislaw will commit himself to work as an "ardent public man" (578), and Dorothea will make for herself a happy life that "radiates" her generous, loving goodness so that "the effect of her being on those around her [will be] incalculably diffusive" (578).

But that conclusion is far into the future: at this point in the novel the compromise is yet to be made. The ground is prepared, however, by their conversation here. Pushing at her earlier notion that Will is still "growing" toward a "vocation" (55), Dorothea says, "I am quite interested in what you will do . . . what your vocation will turn out to be" (155). She suggests "poet." Will knows what a poet must be: he must "have a soul so quick to discern . . . and so quick to feel . . . a soul in which knowledge passes instantaneously into feeling, and feeling flashes back as a new organ of knowledge" (155). Dorothea responds: "I understand what you mean about knowledge passing into feeling." She understands because she already has just such a soul as Will has described: "that seems to be just what I experience" (156).

Dorothea does not expect to write poems, however—"I could never produce a poem"—and she teases Will about forgetting the poems in his talk of the poet. Will's reply is simple, direct, and absolutely central to George Eliot's thesis in this novel: "You *are* a poem," he says (156).

George Eliot is always serious about what art does, and how it works. She is in the great tradition of romanticism as an artist and as a theoretician. Both Dorothea's insistence that art should "make life beautiful . . . everybody's life"—what Will calls "the fanaticism of sympathy" (152)—and Will's own argument that "enjoyment radiates"(153) are part of that tradition and part of George Eliot's faith. When Dorothea and Will can each learn what the other knows—or feels, and as a result of that feeling knows—they will both become whole. To get there, Will teaches Dorothea the way, as best he can—and Dorothea brings Will along with her.

In estimating the worth of an artist George Eliot says that you must ask "what was his individual contribution to the spiritual wealth of mankind." She continues: "Did he impregnate any ideas with a fresh store of emotion?"[36] This key critical idea, of "thought and feeling" at one with each other, is not original with George Eliot. The romantic ideal of such reunification was first expressed by Blake and Wordsworth; it was reiterated in George Eliot's time by several of her contemporaries. Matthew Arnold wrote in praise of poetry that it "thinks. . . . but it thinks emotionally."[37] Walter Pater claimed that "art addresses not pure sense, still less the pure intellect, but the imaginative reason."[38] Douglas Bush, a modern critic, wrote not long ago of Keats's ideas as that kind of "knowledge" which is "a sympathetic understanding of the human condition."[39] Bush's phrase is a good formulation of what George Eliot—and others like her—expect as the result of the combination of thought and feeling.

Shortly after the publication of *Middlemarch*, under the heading "Feeling is a kind of knowledge," George Eliot wrote: "What seems eminently wanted is a close comparison between the knowledge which we call rational and the experience which we call emotional."[40] In the first half of Book 2 we watch Lydgate refusing this thesis: a sort of presumptive schizophrenic, he expects to be able to live separate intellectual and emotional lives. In the second half of the book we are introduced to the argument for the unification of thought and feeling. Here and in the books to follow, we watch Dorothea becoming ever more able to live that kind of wholly understanding life.

Lydgate has his profession, and he is in the process of choosing—more or less consciously—his life. Will is working toward the idea of what to do with his life, though he has chosen as yet no "precise order of occupation"—to use poor Casaubon's words—"to which he would addict himself" (157). Dorothea is much closer to finding her life. But she is Mrs. Casaubon now, not Miss Brooke—and she must return to the world of Middlemarch.

· 7 ·

BEING HEROIC AND CONSTRUCTIVE

It is a long way from Rome to Middlemarch. When we return there at the beginning of Book 3 we have left behind Dorothea's ambition "to make life beautiful" (152) and Will's argument that "the best piety is to enjoy"—and that "enjoyment radiates" (153). Book 3 opens with Fred Vincy worrying about his debts; and for three chapters George Eliot interrupts the novel—or so it seems—with the story of Fred.

One of the things Book 3 does is further set for us the criteria we are to use in judging the novel's characters. The categories given us here are the mercenary and the spiritual. Mercenary life is concerned with quantity, spiritual life with quality. Casaubon, a clergyman, should have a spiritual life—but he does not; instead, he is a "dried-up pedant" (142), "a lifeless embalmment of knowledge" (137). Bulstrode pretends to be a spiritual man, but his true character is that of banker. The Vincys—Mr. and Mrs. Vincy and Rosamond, anyway—are quite simply mercenary, and make no pretense to any other kind of existence.

Fred is a pettily selfish creature most of the time, but he is still likable. Perhaps we manage to like him because Mary Garth does, and she is not one to make mistakes. Perhaps we sympathize with him because he is restless in his idleness, spiritually uncomfortable. As the time for its repayment draws near, his debt bothers him enough that he decides to do something to raise the money that he owes. Caleb Garth has countersigned his note, and Fred realizes to his embarrassment that honest Caleb will pay the money if Fred cannot. He does not think of going to work at anything to earn the money, however; he plans to make it out of nothing—or to make £120 out of a horse not worth half that much, which is the same thing. When he fails at this scheme and comes up without the money, he feels guilty for having taken the Garths' money—and sorry for himself. Neither Garth nor his wife says much to him, so George Eliot sends him to see Mary—who berates him for being "selfish" and useless (175–76). "I am so miserable," Fred says; "if you knew how miserable I am, you would be sorry for me." Mary answers, to the contrary, that "There are other things to be more sorry for" than Fred and his misery; "But selfish people always think their own discomfort of more importance than anything else in the world" (175).

Mary and Fred are an important couple in the novel. We read their interaction here and elsewhere in relation to the interaction of Lydgate and Rosamond, Dorothea and Casaubon, and Dorothea and Will. We must also pay attention to Caleb and Susan Garth, and read the way they live in relation to the way others conduct their lives. The Garths are in some sense George Eliot's model family—and likewise, once Fred has reformed and settled down, he and Mary become George Eliot's model young couple. But to call them models is not to call them central characters. The difference has to do with what George Eliot refers to as "aesthetic teaching" instead of simple didacticism.[41]

The Garths serve as models in a dozen particular instances. Their actions are so often counterparts to the actions of others that sometimes we forget to see them as themselves, and read their lives only for their comparative value and effect. Caleb lends Fred money—and Lyd-

gate borrows from Bulstrode. Caleb quits his work for Bulstrode because, he says, "It hurts my mind" (480); Lydgate cannot quit his
association with Bulstrode and will not admit to problems of conscience. Mary Garth and Dorothea are both concerned with "doing"
and being "useful," and both are aware that—as Mary reminds Fred—
"there are so many things to be done . . . in the world" (176). When
Dorothea gives up Casaubon's money—which she has inherited—in
order to marry Will, we recall the scene at the end of Book 3 in which,
at old Peter Featherstone's death, Mary inadvertently gives up what
might have been Fred's inheritance.

As a family the Garths have a more general significance for the
novel. Every time we meet them we are reminded of the kind of people
they are, and we are invited to use them as models or points of reference for the rest of the novel. Dorothea's idealism, Lydgate's ambition,
Bulstrode's piety, the Vincy family's simple mercenary selfishness,
Will's unfocused energy—all of these traits are set off, in some way, by
contrast with the Garths' honesty and industry.

The Garths are workers, managers, savers. They are principled
people, but they do not flaunt their principles. When you ask a
Garth—Mary, for example—why she does a thing, she will know exactly why. It will not be a whimsical or expedient doing.

Principle and expedience are opposites. To act according to principle means that you have worked out what your values are first and
then act according to those values. Thus Caleb Garth explains that he
"can't be happy in working . . . [or] profiting by" Bulstrode, because
he is "obliged to believe that . . . Raffles has told [him] the truth"
about Bulstrode, that he has "led a harmful life for gain." To continue
as Bulstrode's agent would be to violate principle for Caleb, and that
would hurt his "mind" (480). Expedience, however, would neither
cause nor consider such a problem. Expedience is not concerned with
such things as value. The word means "to get your foot out": *ex* plus
ped, from the Latin *pes* for foot. (You can supply the object—what it
is you get your foot out of.) If, when you get your foot out of the one
mess, you find you have just stuck it into another mess—well, you

jump again, that's all. The most painful example of expedient action in *Middlemarch* is Lydgate's easy acceptance of his involvement with Bulstrode. Given Lydgate's character, such involvement does not hurt his mind at all.

The Garths seem unimportant in the life of Middlemarch—the town, now, not the novel—because of their class. They live "in such a small way," says Mrs. Vincy (160). Caleb works for various people, and both Mary and Mrs. Garth teach children. A woman who has "to work for the bread" (160) is almost a servant in the eyes of the "genteel" world. But being a servant is not such a bad thing. The word servant comes from the Latin *servo*, meaning "to look out for, to save or protect." The Garths serve the rest of Middlemarch—and they and their kind serve us all—by looking out for and protecting our civilization, the idea of society. They are model idealists, Caleb particularly so. He wants things to work right—to be right—in this world.

The great "value" in life, for Caleb, is "that myriad-headed, myriad-handed labour by which the social body is fed, clothed, and housed." His "imagination" is attached to that idea, and his "ambition" has always been "to have as effective a share as possible in that sublime labour" (173). He tried, once, to take too large a share of that "labour," and failed. His failure did not defeat him, however, or cause him to change his ambition or his values. George Eliot so appreciates Caleb's ambition that she dismisses as meaningless—worthless—that the Garth's "lived in a small way" (174). They live useful lives, and contribute to their society by their labors and to ours by their example. "Labour," for George Eliot, is a good thing: and one of Caleb's labors is to turn Dorothea's "plan" into "new farm buildings" for Sir James (161).

The result of Fred's defaulting on his debt means that the Garths end up paying for Fred's amusement with their labor. Their son's apprenticeship—his career in this world of useful labor is to be that of "engineer"—must be postponed or forgone. Seriousness must pay for folly.

Folly always costs in George Eliot's world. Goodness does not always win, nor is evil always punished; she is too much a realist to pretend, sentimentally, to such "silly" nonsense. But she does believe in a system of causal morality, and asserts it in her fiction. At the level of action called "plot" things happen in a more or less random way: Lydgate comes to Middlemarch, instead of going to Southampton or York; Will and Dorothea happen to be in Rome at the same time; Casaubon dies before Dorothea can promise to abide by his secret request. But plot has no meaning and no value. At the more significant level of character, of meaningful human existence, things happen because of who we are and what we do. Lydgate is responsible for his failure in Middlemarch and in life; Dorothea and Will make of their meeting something important to them both; Dorothea must still make her decision about Casaubon's work—and her own life—even though his death saves her from having to tell him, personally, what that decision is.

As George Eliot sees it, we strive, at our best, to control our lives despite the basic randomness of our situation. This is our "Duty," to use her word for the "absolute" necessity of meaningful life.[42] Pursued and performed unstintingly, "Duty" can guarantee meaning for us, but it cannot guarantee what is usually called success. It is true, she says in *Middlemarch,* that "Our deeds are fetters that we forge ourselves"—but it is equally true that "it is the world that brings the iron" (22). Though "there is no creature whose inward being is so strong that it is not greatly determined by what lies outside it" (577), still the heroic creature strives to make a life of meaning despite that limitation: "Our deeds still travel with us from afar," she writes, "And what we have been makes us what we are" (485).

Part of the randomness of the situation in Book 3 of *Middlemarch* is Fred's illness. His gambling is not a "disease"—but he catches a fever when he goes horse-trading in Brassing, "where there [is] gambling on a grander scale" than that at the Green Dragon (463). He falls ill the day after the confession of his failure to the Garths. Just by chance Lydgate happens to be standing outside the Vincy house when Fred needs him, and Mrs. Vincy calls him in to tend her son. That is the plot, and it has—by itself—no significance. But what results from it is quite serious. Lydgate dallies with Rosamond—"they flirted," the narrator remarks—thinking he is in control of the situation. "If a man could not love and be wise," he argues to himself, "surely he could flirt and be wise at the same time" (185). Lydgate discovers that this theory is not true, however, so he makes a "resolution" not to visit the Vincy house again except as Fred's doctor: he chooses to be "wise." But—typical of Lydgate—this choice is only half-serious, and he soon breaks his resolution, deciding "to have a few playful words with Rosamond about his resistance to dissipation" (207). By the end of the scene, Lydgate—"forgetting everything else"—is engaged to be married (208). The man who would be "playful . . . about his resistance to dissipation" is caught in that folly and pays for it.

Just as Lydgate is summoned to the Vincy house on doctor's business, so he makes a professional call to Lowick Manor. But things there are different. Life at Lowick is not at all like life at the Vincy house in Middlemarch, and something different will be expected of Lydgate.

Dorothea and Casaubon are back from Rome, and neither Lowick nor Casaubon measures up to Dorothea's requirements for life. She is "glowing from her morning toilette as only healthful youth can glow"; Casaubon has "risen early complaining of palpitation" (189). Dorothea hopes that "duty" will "present itself in some new form of inspiration and give new meaning" to her situation; but what she sees is "the snow and the low arch of dun vapour," and what she feels is "the stuffy oppression of that gentlewoman's world, where everything was done for her and none asked for her aid" (189). Her "sense of connection with a manifold pregnant existence"—with a living world of possibility—is but "an inward vision"; there are about her no "claims that would have shaped her youthful energies" (189).

Dorothea is useless—as useless as Fred. But whereas Fred is somewhat content in his uselessness, except when Mary scolds him for it, Dorothea wants desperately to be useful. "What shall I do?" is her constant question. She knows, now, that marriage cannot in itself give her either something to do or access to such a something. She knows—senses, feels—that the world is in great need of serious doing, but she does not know anything more than that. Recognizing no other way to proceed, Dorothea decides once more "to go and see her husband, and inquire if she could do anything for him" (190).

Dorothea's desire to help Casaubon is pathetic: his work is useless, and she knows it. He is not a scholar, and we are to expect no "issuing . . . of his mythological key" (192). But Dorothea busies herself at copying out Latin quotations for him anyway. Suddenly, however, she hears a book drop, and sees Casaubon "clinging forward as if he were in some bodily distress." She is needed: there is something to do. And "with her whole soul melted into tender alarm" she asks, "Can you lean on me, dear?" (196). For the first time in her life Dorothea is needed: she must take care of Casaubon. But how? "Help me," she urges Lydgate, when he arrives. "Tell me what I can do." She pleads with him: "Advise me. Think what I can do" (200).

Dorothea sits in "silence . . . though the life within her was . . . intense." Lydgate recommends "foreign travel," perhaps a return to Rome. Dorothea looks "as if she had been turned to marble" (200)—and there she is, in Rome, at the Vatican museum. George Eliot reminds us of that scene, and Dorothea is again "sensuous force controlled by spiritual passion" (132). She explains to Lydgate that Casaubon "minds about nothing else" but his work—and she adds, "And I mind about nothing else" (200). This intense, passionate appeal strikes Lydgate, just as its image struck Naumann, in Rome: "For years after Lydgate remembered the impression produced on him by this involuntary appeal—this cry from soul to soul" (200). He is moved by Dorothea's words, by her somehow sensing or assuming that he and she are "kindred natures [moving] in the same embroiled medium, the same troublous fitfully-illuminated life" (200). Lydgate has no answer for Dorothea's question. He does not know what she can "do." Though he is moved by her "strong feeling" for her husband, he can only reply "that he should see Mr. Casaubon again tomorrow" (200).

The next time Dorothea consults with Lydgate about her husband's health occurs at the beginning of Book 5. She is deeply worried about Casaubon and wants to know how to help him. She seeks Lydgate's professional assistance. He answers her question quickly: "There [are] no signs of change in Mr. Casaubon's bodily condition." Having thus given his professional opinion, Lydgate immediately turns the conversation to his own interest. "Not willing to let slip an opportunity of furthering a favourite purpose" (302), he asks Dorothea for money for his hospital.

Lydgate excuses the "egotistic" aspect of his request as "not [his] fault"—whatever that means! Dorothea responds with her usual selfless generosity: "I shall be quite grateful to you if you will tell me how I can help to make things a little better . . . there must be a great deal to be done" (302). Lydgate then expounds at length on his situation and his ambition. His remarks are a mixture of self-pity and arrogance: "I suppose one must expect to fight one's way. . . . And the ignorance of people about here is stupendous . . . there is no stifling the offence of being young, and a new-comer, and happening to know something more than the old inhabitants" (303).

Dorothea does not complain that the consultation has been turned around, though we certainly must. And though Dorothea does not intend any irony in response to his complaint, we surely hear something like irony in what she says: "How happy you must be, to know things that you feel sure will do good! I wish I could awake with that knowledge every morning" (304).

When Lydgate returns home Rosamond asks him why Dorothea wanted him so urgently. "Merely to ask about her husband's health," the doctor answers; and then, with more excitement and an urgency of his own, he tells her, "I think she is going to be splendid to our New Hospital: I think she will give us two hundred a year" (302).

When Lydgate spoke to Rosamond after his first consultation with Dorothea it was Rosamond who was calculating and mercenary, "thinking" about Dorothea's being "mistress of Lowick Manor, with a husband likely to die soon" (202). Her calculating comes much closer to being excusable than Lydgate's. Rosamond exposes the crassness of her ambition: enough money, to the mercer's daughter, means happiness. Lydgate, however, understands life more largely, and prides himself on his profession as well as on his professional conduct. In his second conversation with Dorothea he violates both with his crassness, with his selfish disregard for Dorothea's purpose in coming to him, and his shamelessly "egotistic" pursuit of his own cause and purpose in return.

It might be argued that Lydgate has every reason to solicit funds for his new fever hospital: after all, it is a worthy project, and will be a "good . . . for Middlemarch" and maybe even "good . . . for the world." And perhaps it could be argued that, unlike poor Lydgate, Dorothea can afford not to worry about money because she is rich: and since she can afford £200, there is nothing wrong with asking her for it. Both arguments fail. The one is confounded by Lydgate's manner. It is not his cause that is wrong, but the way in which he seeks to advance it. The argument about Dorothea's easy situation, her wealth, founders on the rocks of fact that George Eliot gives us about money throughout the novel. Along with everything else in *Middlemarch*, there are lots of sums and figures. Fred's "pleasure-seeking" (163) leaves him £160 in debt. The Garths have less than £110 in savings. It will cost about £90 to apprentice Arthur Garth to an engineer. A good horse costs between £30 and £60. The chaplaincy of the new hospital carries a stipend of £40 a year. Bulstrode's annual contribution to the hospital amounts to £1000. Dorothea's independent income—her inheritance from her own family—comes to £700 a year; she assumes that she and Will can live on that. Lydgate's debt is much larger than Dorothea's "fortune" (560). His extravagance is such that he needs £1000 to fend off his creditors (472). Except as Mrs. Casaubon, Dorothea is not rich. Lydgate has even less—and blaming the world for that mistake, he lives as if he were wealthy.

When Dorothea renounces all that Casaubon has left her so that she can marry Will, she ceases to be rich. At best they can live in modest comfort on £700 a year. Even on his own—unmarried—Lydgate would want more than that; and married to Rosamond he needs several times as much. The important point, however, is not these figures or argument about them. The important point is that money does not matter to Dorothea—or to Will; it is extremely important to Lydgate, however, and to Rosamond.

Book 3 ends as it began, concerned with money. The final chapters are set at Peter Featherstone's house, Stone Court. Just as Rosamond calculated about Casaubon's death and what that would mean to his wife, so all the mercenary clan of Featherstones—including the Vincys—calculate what old Peter's death will mean to them. The Featherstones are comic in their greed and their hypocritical piety. For all that old Peter is a nasty man and a miser, their avarice momentarily converts him into a sympathetic character. We can enjoy his playing with them as he approaches death. They leave Stone Court, at the end of the book, jealously certain that he has left all his money to Mary Garth.

It is ironic, or course, for the Featherstones in their greed to be jealous of Mary. Her ideas and actions give us another contrast to the mercenary attitudes and behavior of old Peter's kin as they hover about, waiting for him to die. Featherstone knows that Mary does not care about money, and in neither of his wills does he leave her anything.

Because Mary is a young woman in Middlemarch—and another young woman in love—we must think of her in comparison to Rosamond and Dorothea. The differences between her and Rosamond are easy, and obvious. Mary is plain, while Rosamond is beautiful. Mary does not want Fred to get an inheritance and be rich; she wants him to find a career and be useful. Rosamond does not really care what Lydgate does as long as he makes a lot of money; to her, in fact, medicine is not "a nice profession" (316)—even if it is a useful one—because it does not bring in enough money. In chapter 31 we watch Rosamond weigh, measure, package, and bind Lydgate—finish her shopping, catch him in her web and prepare to devour him, as George Eliot promised that Middlemarch would. In chapter 33 we see Mary refuse to act in any way which might be construed as self-serving; she will not take Featherstone's money for herself, fearing that it might be some sort of bribe. Rosamond works her will on Lydgate, quite intentionally. Mary—attempting to do what is right—denies old Peter's will, and thwarts him in his last moments by not letting him choose which of his wills to burn; he dies with a heap of useless gold and bank-notes under his hand. Rosamond writes to Lydgate's rich uncle, asking for money. Mary refuses to summon Fred when his rich uncle, dying, asks for him—presumably to give him an inheritance.

What Mary does, of course, is not in any simple sense right or good just because she is not mercenary. She does not even know if what she is doing is right. But she is trying to do the right thing, even when she denies Featherstone his final choice. Rosamond, on the other hand, never thinks of right or wrong; she thinks only of what Rosamond wants for her happiness—and what she wants is what Peter Featherstone dies holding onto: "a heap of notes and gold" (220).

The comparison between Mary and Dorothea is much more difficult. Mary's way of acting is much more genuinely thoughtful than Dorothea's. She doesn't have Dorothea's "ardent" way of seeking the good. Both young women are idealists, but their idealisms—their different forms of idealism—affect the world in different ways, and may elicit different responses from us.

Dorothea's idealism would change the world. Some of us, I suspect, are frightened by her radical ambitions: they might "interfere with political economy and the keeping of saddle-horses" (3). Some of us probably distrust her selflessness, too, and judge it as but another and disguised form of selfishness or pride. But most of us, I hope, admire her for her ambitions. We smile—critically but indulgently—when she makes silly mistakes about jewels or riding. We cringe when she thinks naively of wanting to marry Hooker or Locke or Milton or Pascal, and we wish she would look around her for some nice, bright young man—*if* she wishes to marry. We ache when she marries Casaubon, a man almost as "dead" as any of Dorothea's dead heroes. But we trust Dorothea, still, and we admire her ever-stronger determination to do something good in and for this world.

But Middlemarch does not admire her. From the beginning simple-minded Middlemarchers are "prejudiced against" her "love of extremes" (3), and at the end nobody is pleased that she decides to marry Will. But even when she rejects their way of doing things—their notion of what is right and wrong—she does not really threaten them: they can simply refuse to see or to acknowledge her. If she would become "a queen"—like Sir James "always said [she] ought to be" (566)—they could love her in her difference from them. But they do not—will not—understand her love for Will, or her discovery of her self in love; all they see is what seems to them "poverty," which can only be "uncomfortable" (565–66). "Sane people did what their neighbours did," says Middlemarch wisdom; as for the others, "one might know and avoid them" (3).

It is because of the town's self-protective wisdom that Dorothea is not really dangerous to Middlemarch life. If we examine our own responses to her, we may discover that the same holds true for us as well. For all of her ardent devotion to her ideal of "doing good" and the principle of "making life less difficult to each other" (506) and "mak[ing] life beautiful . . . everybody's life" (152), Dorothea does not really threaten us at all. Our own pettiness, our own bland devotion to inconsequential existence are not endangered by her. George Eliot will insist, at the end of the novel, that Dorothea and others like her do indeed change our lives; but they change our lives the way art does—they "enlarge our sympathies"—not by forcing us to do something, right now.

But Mary Garth, in her plainness and straightforward simplicity, might turn on you or me the same way she turns on Fred, and demand that we get to work and make something of ourselves. Mary is not the kind of ethereal person Dorothea often seems to be. We can neutralize Dorothea, by seeing her as the Virgin Mary, a Christian Antigone, a Saint Theresa, a queen. But Mary is plainly, simply real, and her idealism is immediately active. That is precisely its threat. I sometimes find it difficult in reading *Middlemarch* to judge myself—my life—by her standards. I am not sure I would want her living next door to me.

At the end of the novel "popular opinion" in Middlemarch disarms Mary, and it sighs—with relief—that Dorothea never did the great things that she could have done. I do not think George Eliot intends us to respond to these two women, however, as Middlemarch does. Both Mary and Dorothea are important for the lives they live and the good they do in our world. To George Eliot, our "Duty"—to the beautiful and the good in life—is "peremptory and absolute."[43] Moral perfection is to be found in the beautiful and the good, and that is what she wants to teach us. The Puritan streak in her allows her no room for the beautiful unless it is also good and no room for the good unless it is also useful. "The inspiring principle which alone gives me courage to write," she says, "is that of so presenting our human life as to help my readers in getting a clearer conception and a more active admiration of those vital elements which bind men together and give a higher worthiness to their existence."[44]

There is more to life than "pleasure-seeking" (163), or making money, or prestige. With Mary's help even Fred learns this lesson—and so must we. "I see clearly," George Eliot says, shortly before beginning to write *Middlemarch*, "that we ought, each of . . . to be heroic and constructive."[45]

· 8 ·

Making Life Beautiful

In our society we value and respect philanthropy. If wealthy people give money to the poor, set up libraries, endow chairs at universities, or build wings of hospitals we honor them for their generosity. We honor them—and admire them, too—much more than we honor the people who run the Salvation Army shelter, or who take care of sick people at home, or who in some other quiet way do good in our world. We do not refer to these latter people as philanthropists, "lovers of humanity"; rather, we call them "do-gooders"—and we use that term somewhat pejoratively.

The reason for these attitudes is simple. I can afford to honor and admire philanthropists. I am not rich, so I cannot be expected to give away $10,000 or $100,000. It is safe, therefore, for me to honor those who do. But I could do good, in some quiet way—and therefore "do-gooders" threaten my security and self-respect. I do not have to be rich to help other people; I have no excuse for not doing what the "do-gooders" do. Thus they threaten me, disturb me, trouble my complacency—and I do not like them. Anyway, they are not beautiful people like philanthropists are. "Do-gooders" are generally ugly—like

Mary Garth—and they live ugly, small lives, like she does. If in my fantasies I think of myself as an idealist, I naturally think of being a beautiful one, like Dorothea, who can afford to be philanthropic.

Dorothea and Mary are both idealists, but Mary is much more the practical idealist because she knows the world better, and knows how to work in it. Dorothea has grown up separated from the world and does not know how to do what she sees—or feels—needs to be done. Further, because of her ignorance or her naïveté—because of her inexperience with the world—Dorothea makes mistakes.

It is not that Mary is a realist about marriage and Dorothea is an idealist; on this subject they are both idealists. Mary will not marry Fred until he has found something to do with himself, until he has found a career. She does not say that she will not marry him until he gets a job and starts making money: not at all. In fact Mary insists that she will not marry Fred if he becomes a minister, and she will not marry him if he inherits Peter Featherstone's money. If Fred takes orders and becomes a minister he will be a sham clergyman. If he inherits Featherstone's money he will never do anything useful with his life. As Mary thinks about marriage, she is an idealist: she wants to marry a man who will be in earnest about life. Since she loves Fred, she must therefore try to teach him earnestness and usefulness.

Dorothea wants to be the wife of a serious man, a man who is doing something important and who will teach her how to do something important, too. She is an idealist in that she wants to devote her life to making this world a better place, to doing good and maybe even great things for us all. But she has a limited notion of what marriage can be and almost no notion of what real love is; and she is mistaken in what she regards as doing something important. Thus she marries Casaubon. Her decision to marry Casaubon is not wrong because it is idealistic; it is wrong because it is mistakenly idealistic. She mis-sees and mis-values Casaubon, and mis-sees and mis-values herself.

To maintain that Dorothea mis-values herself is not to suggest that she should learn to be selfish. Philosophically, for George Eliot, self is a means to an end, but never an end in itself. Our society, like her own, pretends to know better than that. Enlightened by progress—or else scared by its disintegration as society—the world we live in believes in self only, and lives the life of self lonely.

Self as a means to an end says, with Dorothea, "What do we live for, if it is not to make life less difficult to each other?" (506). She means that, and so does her creator. We may disagree with them both, but we cannot make either of them say something less than or other than that. We can refuse to listen or to hear, but that is the ultimate selfishness, the ultimate alienation. If I shut out other voices, I lose all touch with reality and end up with a purely subjective view of the world. Me, then, equals the universe.

Let me try to explain—for Dorothea's sake. If I realize that my best happiness will come from trying to make others happy and then set out freely to do good, knowing that the good I do will do me good: that's selflessness. My focus or intent is on doing good and the happiness of others, not on me and my benefits. If I am genuinely selfless, I set out freely to do good for others. The by-product of such action will be good for me: it will yield me my own happiness. If, however, I realize that my happiness will come from trying to make others happy and then set out to do good for others *because* it will make me happy, I am socially dangerous. The end, in this case, is my selfish pleasure, not the accomplishment of good. Eventually, what is good for me may come to determine what I see as good for others. I may learn to corrupt the good I do by making it serve me: "What's good for General Bullmoose," I'll claim, "is good for the country."

That selflessness gives me pleasure—that doing good makes one happy—is the proof of the moral order of the universe. That greed ends, naturally, in frustration—that selfishness ends, naturally, in the frustration of the self—is the corollary to that proof. It's called, in some quarters, the Doctrine of Golden Handcuffs. The last thing I will ever give away to the world—and whether I am selfish or selfless, it will most certainly happen—is my self: in death. In a philosophical sense, then, the only natural, responsible attitude to have in life is the one that prepares the self for its death. Selflessness is the final and most forceful lesson that Nature teaches.

Selflessness does not mean that you do not try to get or do or know the things you want or want to do or want to know. It means, however, that you measure your ambitions socially. Freedom is the great social measure. Etymologically, it is the same word as friendship: they both derive from an old Teutonic word that means "to love." And love, for George Eliot, is the great ambition, even better than making plans or doing good. True love is the "fellowship" (333) that sets us free.

Selflessness also requires that I know myself, and it expects me to act according to that knowledge. Neither ignorance nor moral nonexistence is the same as selflessness. Selfless living implies, necessarily, that I contribute my energy and intelligence socially, for others. I need to know who I am in order to know what I can give that is valuable. It would be destructively antisocial for me to decide to be a selfless physician, and go out twenty-four hours a day offering my medical advice to the poor. I know nothing about medicine; I would kill people with my ignorant generosity. If I simply suppress self and act neutrally in the world—never taking a stand, never making a decision—then I am just taking up valuable space and not paying the rent. If I pretend not to exist as a self—if I hide under a bushel or elsewhere in the dark—I can make no contribution to the world.

All of this takes us—or should—to a discussion of Casaubon. At the beginning of chapter 29, in Book 3, George Eliot announces that she will give us Casaubon's "point of view" (192) for a change. We expect, then, a change in narrative sympathy—but that is not what we get. Rather, we get a change in critical focus. She does not really give us Casaubon's point of view; instead, she turns her attention to him, and analyzes his character and his attitudes. In a sense what she does is to hold up his point of view to her critical analysis—and in so doing she brutalizes the poor man. When she is finished with him she says, wryly, "For my part I am very sorry for him" (193). But that is not pity, or sympathy—and it belittles him still further. He can never "be liberated," she says, from his "small hungry shivering self." His is "an uneasy lot at best": though he is "present at this great spectacle of life," he is doomed "never to have [his] consciousness rapturously transformed into the vividness of a thought, the ardour of a passion, the energy of an action." He will always be "scholarly and uninspired, ambitious and timid, scrupulous and dimsighted" (193).

What brilliant critical pairings those are. Casaubon is scholarly but uninspired, so that his scholarship is but dry and empty pedantry. He is ambitious—his work would be the Key to *All* Mythologies—but timid, afraid of what will be the judgment of others should the fruits of his feeble labors ever be seen. He is scrupulous in his attention to detail, but dimsighted; and thus all his scrupulous work is but a waste of the feeble little energy he has. What a horrible judgment on poor Casaubon! Still, George Eliot does generate sympathy for him, despite what she and her characters—Will, Sir James, Lady Cadwallader—say about him. He is almost beneath contempt, however, as she presents him in the first few paragraphs of this chapter. He is a creature trapped in himself, victimized by a "proud narrow sensitiveness" that George Eliot calls, turgidly, "self-preoccupation or at best egoistic scrupulosity" (193).

When Will writes to Casaubon, Dorothea expects good things: "I can imagine," she says excitedly, "what he has written to you about" (195). Perhaps she thinks Will has written to thank Casaubon for his generous assistance and support. Maybe he is writing to inform Casaubon of his plans to make something of his life, to choose a career or a vocation. He could be telling Casaubon about German scholarship, even, or volunteering to come to Lowick to help in the great work. Whatever it is that Dorothea expects, however, does not matter. Casaubon is jealous of Will, and angry at his letter: "I must decline [his] proposal . . . to pay a visit here. I trust I may be excused for desiring an interval of complete freedom from such distractions as have been hitherto inevitable, and especially from guests whose desultory vivacity makes their presence a fatigue" (195).

Poor Casaubon. He wants "freedom"—from those "distractions" which we would call life. Will's "vivacity" wears him out, causes him "fatigue." Worse yet, Dorothea responds to his pronouncement with energy and anger, and frightens him so much that "his hand tremble[s]" as he tries to work. Furious with "indignation," Dorothea crosses the room to her own desk, and begins to copy out Latin quotations for him. But "her hand [does] not tremble"; the result of her first act of self-assertion is instead a curious kind of calm that soon feels neither "superiority" nor scorn, but does its work instead (196).

Within the hour, Casaubon suffers his first heart attack. Suddenly he is in pain, and Dorothea rushes to him. We realize, then, that even pitiful, petty men can hurt: even Edward Casaubon can feel pain. Despite what we have thought of him, he is in a very real and moving way one of us, another poor human in need of human sympathy. We must marvel, surely, at Dorothea's quick response to him: "Can you lean on me, dear?" (196). She does not stop to consider how he has hurt her or how petty he is. She does not mediate her response to his situation through her earlier "scorn" for him (195); rather, she responds immediately, without the intervention or interposition of self. She responds selflessly to Casaubon's human need, his human pain.

According to the information given us, the cause of Casaubon's heart attack seems to have been the argument he had with Dorothea about Will's coming to visit Lowick. Remembering keenly his response to such a visit, Dorothea asks her uncle to write to Will to prevent his coming. Brooke writes—but as his pen thinks faster than he does, he manages to invite Will, "since he could not be received at Lowick, to come to Tipton Grange" (201).

Brooke intends to use Will as a sort of "secretary" (226) who will "make something" of Brooke's "documents": "I have plenty of ideas and facts, you know, and I can see he is just the man to put them into shape" (225). Casaubon, too, has "documents," but he is afraid of letting anyone help him with them. For all of his pretense to scholarship, his work may have no more significance than Brooke's.

When Will finally comes to pay a call at Lowick, Casaubon happens to be out, and he and Dorothea meet. Dorothea explains how she now tries to "help" Casaubon at his work in small ways and confides to Will the source of that ambition: "when I was a little girl . . . it always seemed to me that the use I should like to make of my life would be to help some one who did great works, so that his burthen might be lighter" (251).

Will suggests that Casaubon should hire a secretary to do such work as Dorothea does, and free her: "you may easily carry help too far," he warns. She responds, "I should have no happiness if I did not help him in his work" (251). Besides, she says, Casaubon "objects to a secretary." Will understands why Casaubon won't tolerate having a secretary: "Mr. Casaubon does not like any one to overlook his work and know thoroughly what he is doing. He is too doubtful—too uncertain of himself" (252). Dorothea recognizes this, too, but still insists on serving her husband. "What could I do?" she asks, if not that; "There is no good to be done in Lowick" (251).

It is in part the limitation of Dorothea's understanding of what she can do that makes her so determined to help Casaubon, and for this—given that she knows the futility of his work—we criticize her. But she also tries to help him because he needs help: he is a stricken, wounded, nearly broken human being.

Dorothea, however, is herself half of Casaubon's wound. As a scholar he has "a passionate resistance to the confession that he [has] achieved nothing," though he knows with "a morbid consciousness" (288) that he is a failure in spite of his claim to "authentic, well-stamped erudition" (289). His "intellectual ambition," characterized now by "a melancholy absence of passion in his efforts at achievement," cannot protect him: it is "no security against wounds, least of all those which [come] from Dorothea" (288). Though she does everything for him, and is "solicitous about his feelings," in his mind he harbors a terrible "certainty that she judge[s] him" and has turned into "the critical wife" (289). George Eliot's response to Casaubon's painful "inner drama" is not sympathetic. His "misery," she says, is "quite ordinary." Its cause is the usual one, selfishness: "Will not a tiny speck very close to our vision blot out the glory of the world? . . . I know no speck so troublesome as self" (289).

Troubled with self, then, Casaubon goes out to wait for Lydgate to come to him—"in the Yew Tree walk," he tells Dorothea, "where I shall be taking my usual exercise." Yews—"sombre evergreens"—are frequently found in cemeteries, and George Eliot describes the Yew-Tree walk at Lowick as a most funereal place where, amid silence and sleeping shadows, even "the cawing of rooks" sounds like "a dirge" (291). There Lydgate informs his patient that he suffers from "fatty degeneration of the heart" (292–93).

Dorothea is not George Eliot, and her response to Casaubon differs from her creator's. Knowing how worried her husband is, Dorothea's sympathetic "impulse" is "to go at once" to him when Lydgate leaves, to try to comfort him. She "might have represented a heaven-sent angel" (254) had Casaubon been capable of seeing such; but his imagination is filled with "the petty anxieties of self-assertion" (293), and cannot see her at all. She "passe[s] her hand through his arm," hoping to touch him to response; but "Mr. Casaubon kept his hands behind him," and only "allowed her pliant arm to cling with difficulty against his rigid arm." When they return to the house, Dorothea releases his arm, "that she might leave her husband quite free." He shuts himself up in his library, "alone with his sorrow" (294).

Dorothea's anger at Casaubon's rejection of her solicitude turns her usual question about "doing" into a critical analysis of her attempt at married life with him: "What is the use," she asks herself, "of anything I do?" (294). She struggles with this question, knowing easily the answer to one part of it—that helping him with his work is helping him in vain—but in great difficulty as to the answer to the other part, which concerns her life with him as both her husband and a feeling, hurting human being.

We might expect—might even hope for—some sort of declaration of independence from Dorothea at this point. But "the noble habit of the soul reasserts itself" in her, George Eliot says, and Dorothea resolves her difficulty by deciding to go to him again, to attempt a second time to be of "use" to him. She weighs her "anger" at him against her sense that he has asked Lydgate about his future, and that Lydgate's answer "must have wrung his heart." That was the "conviction" with which she first walked out to meet Casaubon after Lydgate's departure. Now it returns to override her anger with sympathy, and she goes out onto the stairs to wait for him to quit his solitude.

Dorothea knows what she is doing. Her decision to try again to help her husband—to assist him in whatever way he can let himself be assisted—is the result of "knowledge passing into feeling," which she earlier told Will is so often her "experience" (156). And what she feels, now, as she takes her husband's hand, is "the thankfulness that might well up in us if we had narrowly escaped hurting a lamed creature" (296).

The ancient Greeks had a motto that said, in the usual modern translation, that wisdom comes through suffering: παθέι μάθος, in Aeschylus's *Agamemnon*.[46] The word that translates as "suffering," however, has a more general meaning of "feeling," or "feeling through experience"; the largest, most significant meaning of the phrase, for the ancient Greeks as well as for us, might well be that wisdom comes through feeling, or through learning how to feel. Our word sympathy comes from this same Greek word, πάθος, and with the prefix συμ it means "to feel with" or "to feel together with."

Dorothea's sympathy for Casaubon derives from her understanding of his pain. But sympathy for the lame and wounded is often tedious and destructive, for all of one's understanding, and it may not be altogether wise. Dorothea wants for herself "work which would be directly beneficent, like the sunshine and the rain," but her sympathy has committed her "to live more and more in a virtual tomb," doing "ghastly labour [that] would never see the light" (329).

Casaubon's "petty anxieties of self-assertion" (293) force him at last to involve Dorothea fully in his work. In his fear of empty death he starts to order his work and proposes to Dorothea her "intelligent participation in [his] purpose." She knows now, however, that the work is worthless, and she understands the purpose of the "sifting process" (329) he is now beginning. He is anxious that she "observe . . . the principle on which [his] selection is made"—and she feels "sick at heart" (330). Dorothea knows that Casaubon expects her to continue his barren labors after his death.

How far must Dorothea's sympathy take her? Will regards her life at Lowick as a "dreadful imprisonment" and says so. She responds by claiming to have "no longings. . . . for [her]self," and she defends the smallness of her life with her "belief" in "desiring what is perfectly good, even when we don't quite know what it is and cannot do what we would." By so desiring the good, she maintains, we are "widening the skirts of light" (270). Such radiance, she argues, is not just her religion, it is her "life" (271). But how much radiant life can Dorothea have, laboring in a "virtual tomb"? Though she may not "quite know" what the good is, she does know that the "Key to All Mythologies" will "never see the light" or deserve to. If she truly "desire[s] what is perfectly good," she cannot pursue—willfully—what is not good.

When Casaubon proposes to Dorothea that she pledge to carry out his as yet unspoken wishes after his death, she sees his request as "a new yoke for her." She knows that the "sifting" he would have her do is useless: his work is but "the doubtful illustration of principles still more doubtful . . . on which he had risked all his egoism," and she sees herself wasting "days, and months, and years" of her life in "sorting what might be called shattered mummies" (331). But then her "pity" turns "from her own future to her husband's past . . . [and] present." She adopts his perspective, sympathetically—we may remember the narrator's earlier comment about how we see things: "but why always Dorothea? Was her point of view the only possible one with regard to this marriage?" (192). Dorothea thinks of Casaubon's "lonely labour," his "ambition" and "self-distrust," and now his fear of impending death. And for herself, she recalls that she "wished to marry him that she might help him in his life's labour" (332).

Dorothea understands Casaubon's selfishness, his baseness: though she does not say it, she knows that her once "affable archangel" is but "a poor creature" (196). Still, she tries to imagine some more honorable thing that he may want to bind her to—something decent, something other than continued work at his worthless scholarship—but she cannot "believe" in the possibility. He wants only to chain her to his failure. She knows him: "his heart [is] bound up with his work only" (332), and he has no heart for anything else.

Dorothea asks herself, then, "Was it right, even to soothe his grief," to sacrifice her life to him? But she also asks herself whether she could deny him—whether she could say, "I refuse to content this pining hunger?" (332). When the time comes to give him his answer, Dorothea feels certain that she will say "yes"—but not out of strength of character, or belief in the rightness of such a choice. Rather, she will say "yes" because she is "too weak, too full of dread at the thought of inflicting a keen-edged blow on her husband, to do anything but submit completely" (333).

Dorothea has not yet found the strength to assert herself for what she knows is right, and to stand by her self-assertion. Her sympathy for Casaubon is both right and good, but her submission to his selfishness is wrong and bad. She asserted herself against him earlier, and this act freed her, momentarily. In that moment of freedom she saw him stagger, stricken, and then gave him her sympathy. We marveled then at her generosity and her goodness. The present situation, however, is different. She is "compelled" to accept Casaubon's will by "her own compassion" and "her husband's nature." His "nature" is perverse and would take advantage of her compassion to enslave her.

For Dorothea to "soothe his grief" at dying by relinquishing her own life is not "right" at all. Such "right" went out of moral favor when living wives stopped being buried with their dead husbands. Dorothea is saved from such a fate only by George Eliot's intervention: Casaubon dies before she can make her terrible promise.

After Casaubon's death, Dorothea returns—again—to her usual preoccupation with "what she ought to do." Now it is as "the owner of Lowick Manor" that she wishes "to exert [her]self" (338): "There are so many things which I ought to attend to," she says; "Why should I sit . . . idle?" (340). She seems to have learned something from her narrow escape. Though she still values "faithfulness" as a "supreme use," and knows that if she had made that dreadful pledge to Casaubon, out of "pity," she would have kept it, she also recognizes Casaubon for what he was, and sees herself, now, as she was when his wife: a woman under "painful subjection" to a selfish—though also "suffering"—man (342).

Dorothea is more ready now to "do" things than she has been earlier in the novel. She knows more: what she "feels" now comes more from her "experience," and becomes much more trustworthy as a kind of "thought" (156). Her new knowledge will enable her to think more toward the large world, as well: she is more nearly ready for "going into society" (7). When Celia argues against her return to Lowick—"What will you do at Lowick, Dodo? You say yourself that there is nothing to be done there"—Dorothea replies that she plans to explore more largely now and hopes to act in a larger world: "I wish to know . . . what there is to be done in Middlemarch" (370).

Saying this, Dorothea becomes for the first time a truly serious threat to local order. No one took her seriously when, as Miss Brooke, she drew plans. But now she is a wealthy and independent-minded widow. Casaubon tried to restrict her freedom, both with the pledge he tried to elicit before he died and with the will that he left behind him. Mrs. Cadwallader, too, tried to restrain her, arguing against Dorothea's "always . . . taking things sublimely." Almost quoting George Eliot's wry comment about the voice of society in the opening chapter, Mrs. Cadwallader tells Dorothea: "We have all got to exert ourselves a little to keep sane, and call things by the same names as other people call them by." Dorothea answers with her independence: "I never called everything by the same name that all the people about me did," she says; "I still think that the greater part of the world is mistaken about many things. Surely one may be sane and yet think so" (371).

In her new freedom, Dorothea is contemplating doing great things—"interfer[ing] with political economy" (3) even. Her rejection of conventional sanity can perhaps be effective now: no longer must she restrict herself to drawing plans, or to merely symbolic acts of defiance to restrictive customs. Mrs. Cadwallader is not worrying about political economy, however, or even the waste of a good fortune on model housing for the poor; her mind is on Will Ladislaw, and the scandal that must occur should Dorothea decide to marry him.

When Dorothea moves back to Lowick, she begins by settling, finally, the matter of her relationship with Casaubon. She acts as though he were still alive: she carries on her thoughts "as if they were a speech to be heard by her husband." She still feels "the pity which had been the restraining compelling motive in her life with him," but she also judges him, and tells him "in indignant thought . . . that he was unjust" (372). And then she closes up inside the *Synoptical Tabulation for the use of Mrs. Casaubon* a message for him: "*I could not use it. Do you not see now that I could not submit my soul to yours, by working hopelessly at what I have no belief in?*" (372).

Focusing her freedom, Dorothea thinks of Will and wants to see him. She does believe in him— in his "growing" and in his finding someday his "vocation" (55). When she sees him, he seems to have found it: "There will be a great deal of political work to be done by-and-by," he says, "and I mean to try and do some of it" (374). Dorothea replies with delight that he now seems to care, not just for "poetry and art"—and enjoyment—but "about the rest of the world" as well (374–75).

Will and Dorothea are more alike now than they were before. Neither of them knows yet exactly what to do in or for this world, but they both feel strongly that such doing is what they want most in life. Were it not for Will's "pride" (376) he could probably admit that even more than doing things, he wants Dorothea to love him. Dorothea, on her part, is not yet aware that she loves Will, though she does want there to be an "active friendship between them" (377). Were Will to tell her of his love, she would probably recognize her own. But Will is not as great or as selfless as Dorothea; and their love, then, must wait until Dorothea asserts it, claims it for them both, before it can be complete.

The most remarkable, beautiful thing in *Middlemarch* will be Dorothea's discovery that she loves Will. That she gives up a fortune to marry him is insignificant; that she gives herself to him, freely, and takes him in return, is wonderful. That two people who are serious about life can go into the world together to "do" something "to make life beautiful" (152) is more than good, for George Eliot—and much more than philanthropy. It is love: and love, even more so than enjoyment, "radiates" (135).

Even when she was Will's and Dorothea's age, George Eliot believed in "the *truth of feeling* as the only universal bond of union."[47] When Celia wonders "how it . . . came about" that her sister fell in love with Will and decided to marry him, Dorothea answers, cryptically, "If you knew how it came about, it would not seem wonderful to you." And she explains: "you would have to feel it . . . else you would never know" (567).

• 9 •

REFORM

When Will returns from Rome to Middlemarch, at Brooke's invitation, he quickly becomes involved in politics—and so, for a while, does *Middlemarch*. From the very beginning of the novel politics has been a large part of the context within which its inhabitants live. George Eliot warns us, for example, that Dorothea's idealism might upset "political economy" (3), and Brooke—who "knew Wilberforce" and has himself been asked to go "into Parliament" (10) agrees: "Young ladies don't understand political economy, you know" (9). Sir James, though politically conservative, has been reading Davy's *Agricultural Chemistry* to "see if something can't be done" to reform farming for his tenants (8). Over her uncle's objections, Dorothea endorses Sir James's good intentions: "It is not a sin to make yourself poor in performing experiments for the good of all" (9). Brooke collects "documents on machine-breaking and rick-burning" (15)—both socially and politically serious issues of the time—and Mr. Vincy worries about "Parliament going to be dissolved, and machine-breaking everywhere" (243). The "Catholic Question" comes up in the opening chapter, and again in chapters 4 and 6, and Mrs. Cadwallader teases

Brooke about his "politics," and being "put up" for Parliament "on the Whig side" (34).

Though Lydgate is not interested in politics, he comes to Middlemarch talking of "medical reforms" and presents himself "as a reformer" (84). His profession, as he sees it, "wanted reform" (99). George Eliot tells us that "at the end of 1829," when the novel opens, "most medical practice was still strutting or shambling along the old paths"; Lydgate, "a spiritual young adventurer," plans to introduce "reforms" (100, 101), despite the resistance of his colleagues who consider "reform" a "humbug" (107). To Lydgate's mind, "there must be all sorts of reform soon" in the medical profession, and then "young fellows may be glad to come and study" his new ways with him (313). But though Lydgate is "always obtruding his reforms" (126), he is "no radical in relation to anything but medical reform" (240).

Toward the beginning of Book 4, George Eliot brings Will back to Middlemarch and attaches him to the idea of reform by putting him to work for Brooke as editor of the "Pioneer" and Brooke's political advisor. Concerned with the question of parliamentary reform and what eventually became the Reform Bill of 1832, the theme now takes on a capitalized significance as that of "Reform" (249). The times are agitated and unsettling; Parliament is to be dissolved, and a general election called. Everybody, suddenly, is concerned with "Reform."

Middlemarch is set between 1829, the year the "Catholic Question" is settled by the Emancipation Act in Parliament, and 1832, the year of the Great Reform Bill. In 1871, when George Eliot was writing *Middlemarch,* a second Great Reform Bill had just been passed, and Reform was again—or still—a timely issue. In some ways the first Great Reform Bill—the main provisions of which were the extension of franchise and the parliamentary recognition of forty-two previously unrepresented boroughs—might be said to mark the entry of Britain into the modern age. The Industrial Revolution was already in its third generation in England, which was in part what made reform necessary: the recent history of "machine-breaking" and "rick-burning" to which Brooke refers (15) was a direct response to the introduction of new technology to farming and the manufacturing industries. Though there had been no revolution in Britain during the eighteenth century, as there had been in France and elsewhere, things were "going on a little fast," as Brooke observes (264). Everyone in Britain, it seems, knew that major changes had to be made in the system of national governance and in the manner of British life. But many people opposed such change personally, even though they recognized the need for it nationally. And many more were terrified of what such change would mean for themselves and for England. There was not much doubt, however, that change was inevitable; the question was whether or not it was to be instituted by law, as "reform."

Similar arguments, fears, and realizations struck many Englishmen in the years leading up to the second Reform Bill of 1867. For many would-be prophets this second extension of democracy could mean nothing other than the end of British civilization. Thomas Carlyle, himself an ardent and noisy reformer in his younger days, attacked the 1867 Reform Bill furiously. In "Shooting Niagara—And After?" he presented the extension of franchise in apocalyptic terms: "Democracy," he prophesied, would "complete itself disastrously," and religion would be replaced by "Free Trade" in the "Cheap and Nasty."[48]

By 1871 worry about the success of Britain's most recent great experiment in democracy was not yet quelled or silenced. Though Benjamin Disraeli, a Tory, introduced the bill and guided it through Parliament, it was a stronger, more radical Reform Bill than he had wanted. The Tory government fell the following year.

In 1866, the year before the second Reform Bill, George Eliot wrote *Felix Holt the Radical*. Like *Middlemarch* five years later, *Felix Holt* is set in the time of the first Reform Bill. *Felix Holt* is often referred to as George Eliot's "political" novel, but it is finally no more political than *Middlemarch*. The plot is certainly more directly involved with politics, but neither the values, judgments, and conclusions nor the aesthetic life of the novel has anything to do with politics. Indeed, its theme is at least in part that political reform matters far less than personal reform. The Reverend Mr. Lyon tells Felix, "you glory in the name of Radical, or Root-and-branch man"; Felix answers, continuing the etymological pun, "A Radical—yes; but I want to go to some roots a good deal deeper down than the franchise."[49]

Reform is a thoroughly congenial theme for George Eliot, philosophically. An ardent, serious woman, she believes with absolute conviction in the cause of human improvement. In *Felix Holt* as in *Middlemarch*, "radicalism" is the cause adopted by those who have "hopes for the world" rather than for themselves. Felix is "wedded to poverty," he says, "because it enables me to do what I want to do on earth"—which is simply "to try to make life less bitter for a few within my reach." [50]

George Eliot uses the context of political reform in both *Felix Holt* and *Middlemarch* to generalize the theme of reform for us. She is not writing historical fiction. Reform for her is not a matter of politics or intrigue or power; it is a matter of duty and understanding and principle. She would have agreed with John Ruskin, her contemporary, that "political economy" was morally worthless as but "the investigation of the phenomena of commercial operations."[51] She would have despised, I am sure, the amazingly simple discovery by the Nobel-prize-winning economist that many politicians act out of selfishness, or self-interest. She would have despised this allegedly scientific discovery not because it is not true, but because the Nobel laureate who made it is not concerned with its ramifications for decent existence. Ruskin claimed that "political economy," properly understood, was concerned with "the support of [the state's] population in a healthy and happy life"; its end, he said, should be "the service of man."[52] George Eliot would have agreed.

"What do we live for," Dorothea asks—for George Eliot—"if it is not to make life less difficult to each other?" (506). Because we have accepted "political economy" as something much less than that ideal, our society is in need of reform. Both its structure and its institutions need reform—but first we must reform ourselves, personally and individually. We must reform values: then we can change society.

"Economy" is a good word, despite what it means today. In our

time economics is but a descriptive—and valueless—science that explains at the most simple level possible how humans deal with material
things. As an understanding of human social existence, Marxism fails
because it is a materialist response to capitalist materialism. Philosophically, George Eliot was neither a capitalist nor a Marxist. For
her, what was important about life was not material success or gain.
Neither Vincy values—and Rosamond's are but an extension of her
father's—nor Lydgate nor Bulstrode values are worth anything. Again,
George Eliot would have agreed with Ruskin: "There is no Wealth but
Life." [53]

"Economics" means something like "how we manage things at
home." Οἶκος is the Greek word for "home"; νομός the word for
custom or law. Once upon a time, the assumption inherent in the word
was that we were all in this thing called life together, not in competi-
tion against each other. Dorothea stands for such an assumption and
makes it her ideal. So does Will, in a slightly different way.

Dorothea's determination to live by her ideals is what makes *Middlemarch* such a great novel. In that determination lies her heroism.
Set in context with all the reform activity of her time, amid all the
various reformers, she emerges finally as the most radical of them all.
Her ambition is not just to enlarge the political franchise; she urges
us, instead to enlarge our human sympathies.

In 1871 Englishmen were accustomed to hearing the clamor for
reform; they had been hearing it, almost without interruption, for
nearly twenty years. But few Englishmen were sympathetic to what
they heard, and fewer still were willing to live by such sympathies.
Their failure reflected not so much wickedness, blindness, or stupidity.
Rather it derived from that other source of our undoing, called the
refusal to take life seriously all the time.

George Henry Lewes, George Eliot's husband, loved *Middlemarch*. But he would have shocked Dorothea with his attitudes toward
the publication of her novel. And if Caleb Garth had been a publisher,
he would very likely have resigned: Lewes's ideas would have "hurt
[his] mind" (480). Lewes was George Eliot's businessman. In making

the publishing arrangements for *Middlemarch* he suggested to William Blackwood, among other things, "an advertisement sheet bound up with each part," explaining that this "would not only bring in some hard cash, it would help to make the volume look bigger for the 5/-" price.[55] Again, a few days later, he explains to Blackwood that "The part must not *look thin* for 5/- and we must therefore see how many handsome pages it will make."[56] One response to Lewes's worry about the "thin" part, proposed by Blackwood's London manager, was the use of "paper . . . of a loose spongy texture so as to give thickness to the volume." "The public want quantity for their money," he explained, "but might be satisfied with the appearance of it."[57]

Dorothea would object to such trickery, surely, and so would Garth. Brooke would not, however; it would have made easy sense to him. Like most of the rest of us who do not take life very seriously, he would see no wrong in such petty wrongdoing. For George Eliot—at least for George Eliot the author of *Middlemarch*—those attitudes that accept petty wrongdoing are what need first to be reformed. From George Eliot's point of view, reform is simple—and quite radical: we must learn to take our own lives seriously and live them intending both to be good and to do good for others. To add such a difficult requirement to the already difficult list of reforms on the political and social agenda for an Englishman in 1871 might have been more than he could have accepted. Popular opinion—even intelligent popular opinion—was not convinced that civilization would survive what had happened in 1867. Agitation for yet more reform would not have been a congenial topic for the times.

But civilization had survived the first Great Reform Bill, which seemed to the prosperous survivors, looking back from the vantage point of history, not to have been such a bad thing after all. By setting her novel in the time of that earlier, now completed struggle, George Eliot manages to speak to her readers' serious current interest without causing them great anxiety. Even if they are not eager for more reform now, they can look back sympathetically at the need for reform some forty years before. And if they can sympathize with the reforms that worked—or seemed to have worked—in political and social life, perhaps they will also learn to sympathize with those greater reforms that George Eliot proposes for their personal lives, by accepting Dorothea's idealism.

The same kind of argument can be made for us, I suspect, as that just outlined for George Eliot's nineteenth-century readers. Our world may not be quite perfect yet, though we have made a great deal of progress—or so it is said. Agitation for reform is still with us, however, and many of us are frightened by the zealous reformers who would further change our world. But we believe in democracy, and agree absolutely with the provisions of the first Reform Bill. We are sympathetic, too, to what Lydgate saw as the need for reform in his profession, and as enlightened moderns we do not find it very hard to accept Sir James's notion that "one is bound to do the best for one's land and tenants" (263). If we are not careful, however, we will be moved by Dorothea's radiant goodness—and we might even sympathize with her when she says, "What do we live for, if it is not to make life less difficult to each other?" (506). Someday, perhaps, we may find those words inscribed over the doors to the bank, or printed as a motto on our dollar bills.

Middlemarchers are critical of Brooke for his "flirtation with politics"—not because he is a reformer, but because he is "the most retrogressive man in the county" (262). Though Brooke has hired Will to edit his newspaper, and Will is genuinely interested in reform, Brooke is himself one of the people in Middlemarch who needs most to be reformed. He is a terrible landlord. Sir James's argument that "one is bound to do the best for one's land and tenants" (263) turns back from Brooke the would-be politician to Brooke the Middlemarcher, and it turns the theme of Reform back to that of reform. "If I were Brooke," says Mrs. Cadwallader, "I would . . . [get] Garth to make a new valuation of the farms, and [give] him *carte blanche* about gates and repairs: that's my view of the political situation" (266). Brooke's "speechifying to the Middlemarchers" and other political activities "don't . . . signif[y] two straws," Cadwallader continues; "But it does signify about the parishoners in Tipton being comfortable" (267).

When Brooke accosts tenant farmer Dagley about his small son's poaching a leveret, Dagley threatens him with "the Rinform" (274). We know the significance of the scene for the novel from the context George Eliot has built for it. This world of ours is in need of immediate reform. And the kind of reform needed is human and personal first— and then, if necessary, governmental and political: that is what democracy depends on. Little things first, George Eliot argues, and then big things. Brooke should know what needs to be done, even without "the Rinform."

Poor Brooke, in his stupidity, does not mind Dorothea's drawing plans for cottages—"it was quite your hobby," he tells her, shortly before going to Dagley's hovel. But Brooke does not want Dorothea "getting too learned for a woman" (268)—and interfering, perhaps, with "political economy." Dorothea does not object to this slur, but George Eliot does, indirectly, by letting Dorothea speak at length against Brooke's ignorance and for reform. She begins cautiously enough, informing her uncle that "Sir James . . . is in hope of seeing a great change made soon in the management of [Brooke's] estate." Then, speaking for herself, she tells Brooke what he must do and why. She speaks to her uncle as to a man who is running for Parliament; but the values and principles she articulates are hers, and what she says is directed at the landowner who stands in front of her, not the prospective member for Middlemarch:

> "you mean to enter Parliament as a member who cares for the improvement of the people, and one of the first things to be made better is the state of the land and the labourous. Think of Kit Downes, uncle, who lives with his wife and seven children in a house with one sitting-room and one bed-room hardly larger than this table!—and those poor Dagleys, in their tumble-down farmhouse, where they live in the back kitchen and leave the other rooms to the rats! That is one reason why I did not like the pictures here, dear uncle—which you think me stupid about. I used to come from

the village with all that dirt and coarse ugliness like a pain within me, and the simpering pictures in the drawing-room seemed to me like a wicked attempt to find delight in what is false, while we don't mind how hard the truth is for the neighbours outside our walls. I think we have no right to come forward and urge wider changes for good, until we have tried to alter the evils which lie under our own hands."

(268–69)

Brooke's "masculine consciousness" is reduced, George Eliot says, to "a stammering condition under the eloquence of his niece." She is much too "learned" for Brooke, and much too courageously human. He complains, defensively, that she is too "ardent" and "a little one-sided" (269).

Will is present in this scene, having been with Brooke when Dorothea came to Tipton—and she came, we know, at Sir James's request, to present her argument to her uncle. When Dorothea enters, Will is "ridiculously disappointed" that she has come not to see him but with a larger purpose in mind. When she finishes with Brooke, Will's "masculine consciousness" is also affected by her "eloquence" at first, and he retreats momentarily from her "greatness." He recovers his better sense, however, and promises immediately they are alone, "now I have heard you speak . . . I shall not forget what you have said" (269).

When Dorothea and Will are together they always talk about serious things. This time it is "religion." Dorothea tells Will that her sustaining "belief" is in "desiring what is perfectly good" (270). Will's is "To love what is good and beautiful when I see it" (271). Dorothea is Will's inspiration; she is both good and beautiful in his eyes, and he is her "worshipper" (300). It would be sacrilege to call Lydgate's attachment to Rosamond worship; Rosamond is not worthy of such, nor is Lydgate's affection for her appropriately serious. But Will is "devout" in his response to Dorothea. When Rosamond asks him, "What is it that you gentlemen are thinking of when you are with Mrs. Casaubon?" Will answers, "Herself." And he explains, then: "When one sees a perfect woman, one never thinks of her attributes—one is conscious of her presence" (300).

It is not just Dorothea's perfection, however, that works on Will; there is also potential in Will—the potential that Dorothea recognized or believed in when she first met him. When Lydgate is with Dorothea he thinks of her money—"she will give us two hundred a-year" (302) because he is a selfish, mercenary man. When Will sees her he "thinks [not] of her attributes," much less of her money; he is "conscious," rather of "her presence" (300).

Will stays in Middlemarch in order to be near Dorothea. His work for Brooke is but his public excuse for remaining there. "It is undeniable," George Eliot says, "that but for the desire to be where Dorothea was, and perhaps the want of knowing what else to do, Will would not at this time have been meditating on the needs of the English people or criticising English statesmanship" (318). But his work for Brooke is real work, and he begins "thoroughly to like" it and to "stud[y] the political situation with as ardent an interest as he had given to poetic metres or [Pre-Raphaelite] mediaevalism" (318). Will's new interest seems to tend toward seriousness at last, and George Eliot remarks, approvingly: "Our sense of duty must often wait for some work which shall take the place of dilettanteism and make us feel that the quality of our action is not a matter of indifference" (318–19). Working with Brooke on "Reform" (317), Will begins to reform himself for Dorothea.

Will is still uncomfortable being "harnessed" (324) to Brooke: it is difficult to dedicate yourself to principle while working for a man who has barely the intellectual gravity to say the word. Eventually the harness breaks: Brooke gives up the race, and sells the "Pioneer" (352). Once earlier in their association Brooke—forgetting in his usual soft-headed way that one of the objects of Reform is to abolish pocket-boroughs—has wished that "somebody had a pocket-borough to give . . . Ladislaw" (318). Now, freed from Brooke, Will dreams his own dreams of political life for himself, "of wonders that he might do . . . political writing, political speaking would get a higher value now public life was going to be wider and more national" (351). The end of such "distinction," of course, would be his winning the right to ask Dorothea to marry him. As he prepares to leave Middlemarch, he tells her his plan: "There will be a great deal of political work to be done by-and-by, and I mean to try and do some of it" (374).

The difference between Dorothea and Will is that Dorothea is anxious to work for the good, even when she does not know what to do: her "sense of duty" does not wait for the "work" to appear. Will, however, is "dilettanteish" (132); were it not for Dorothea's inspiration he might never find the "work which . . . [takes] the place of dilettanteism" and gives meaning to life (318–19).

The story George Eliot weaves together with Will's and Dorothea's throughout Book 4 and again in Book 6 is the parallel story of Fred and Mary. It begins with Caleb Garth's being asked to undertake the management of Sir James's and Brooke's estates, and part of Casaubon's (277). Caleb's great pleasure in life is work: the worst thing he can imagine is "to sit on horseback and look over the hedge at the wrong thing, and not be able to put [his] hand to it and make it right" (279). This new work will give him the opportunity of "putting men into the right way with their farming, and getting a bit of good contriving and solid building done—that those who are living and those who come after will be the better for." So pleased is Caleb at this prospect that he would "sooner have it than a fortune" and "would be glad to do it for nothing" (278).

With this added responsibility, Garth will "want help by-and-by" (278). Farebrother tells him that Fred is going back to Cambridge to finish his degree—because "he doesn't know what else to do" (279). Soon Garth's musing mind settles on Fred, and he tells his wife, "I am thinking I could do a great turn for Fred Vincy . . . it might be the making of him into a useful man" (282–83).

Fred comes home with his degree (354) in Book 5, but with no better understanding of what he might do with his life than he had before. His "efforts to imagine what he was to do" are all unsuccessful, partly because of the qualifications he has listed for the job: it must be "gentlemanly, lucrative, and to be followed without special knowledge" (384).

Suddenly, by accident, Caleb needs Fred's assistance: "What have you got to do today, young fellow?" he asks. Fred replies, "Nothing" (385). The work he does, then, with Garth becomes "pleasure," partly because to Fred's mind he is "courting Mary when he [is] helping her father" (385). As he works Fred begins "to shape an employment for himself" that has none of the attractions he had earlier regarded as necessities; and forgetting his expectations of some kind of "gentle-manly" and "lucrative" work which he can do without any sort of training, Fred asks, "Do you think that I am too old to learn your business, Mr. Garth?" Encouraged by Garth, he asks, "You do think I could do some good at it, if I were to try?" (387).

When Caleb tells Susan that he is going to "take [Fred] and make a man of him," he is pleased with himself—not selfishly, but because he has found an opportunity to do good for someone else in this world. And even then, Caleb scarcely claims the good done as his own. Just as Dorothea inspires Will to do good just by being herself, so Mary helps Fred, according to Garth: "The lad loves Mary, and a true love for a good woman is a great thing, Susan. It shapes many a rough fellow" (389).

Fred's reform is both Mary's and Caleb's doing. It is beautiful and satisfying—but it is not grand or heroic. Caleb's wisdom is much like Dorothea's idealism, but Caleb's life is seasoned by labor and respon-sibility, and by circumstances which, though they do not limit him spiritually, certainly cramp him physically and economically. Mary knows that she "would never marry an idle, self-indulgent man" (389)—and she knows that she loves Fred, but she does not know the possibility of dreams as great as those that animate Dorothea. Fred's discovery of a worthy life takes him back to the land, to work with his hands as well as his head. Whereas Will's work will take him to London, and involve him in the great large world of "politics," the focus of Fred's labor will be the management, someday, of "a few hundred acres" (279).

The world that Fred learns to inhabit usefully and productively is not, however, smaller or less significant than Will's. They both work in this one world. Their work is different, but their worlds are the same world. We see this, briefly, in the scene which leads up to Garth's first pressing Fred into his service. What brings Fred and Garth together is a contest between suspicious farmers and intrusive railway surveyors: the large modern world is enroaching upon Middlemarch, and the threat that we call progress begins already to mingle itself with that other thing called reform (381).

The railroad is just one more thread, or pair of threads, woven into the immense fabric of this novel. *Middlemarch* is, as George Eliot wanted it to be, "a panoramic view of provincial life."[58] It is not, however, the wide panorama which impresses us as we read, but the depth of the insight into human lives, and the richness of the meaning of life which results from the weaving together of the whole.

Middlemarch is a novel about industrial progress and agricultural improvement and the state of medical knowledge, about the function of the clergy and education and economics, about moral issues ranging from selfishness and greed to what might be called murder, about politics and political reform and doing something useful, about the good and the beautiful. It is also about individual human beings living their lives. And with Fred and Mary, as with Dorothea and Will, it is about that great thing which reforms—or could reform—all our lives, called love.

· 10 ·

SELFISHNESS

Book 5 of *Middlemarch* is entitled "The Dead Hand." In this chapter I will focus on that book as much as possible. We will be concerned with the weight of that dead hand—Casaubon's—on the living present through the effect of his last will. We will also be interested in the adventures of Will Ladislaw. And to complete the pun, we will have to argue about volition and free will.

So far we have set up an examined several themes in *Middle-march*: reform, freedom, the relationship between thought and feeling, art and sympathy, and love. We have not completed our examination of any of these themes, of course—and we will not until we can bring them all back together and call them by their collective name, *Middlemarch*.

George Eliot started out with "Miss Brooke" and *Middlemarch*; in the end she wrote eight parts—eight "books"—to make "Miss Brooke" and *Middlemarch* one. That is what we have to do as readers, and we do it not just by recollecting or uniting the somewhat artificial divisions of the novel into eight parts, but by uniting or reuniting—forming or reforming—the various themes of the novel into a great whole.

The whole is the sum of its parts, to be sure, as well as more than that sum. Each of the characters we have discussed so far has a sense, more or less free, of his or her world or environment. Each of us lives at the center of a small world. An "environment" is what I call that which surrounds me. It is perhaps difficult, as environmentalists in this sense, not to be egotists: difficult not to regard our own little worlds as the only worlds, difficult to remember that ours are not the only seeing eyes.

One way we escape the egotism of such a restricted point of view is by trying to be objective. We insist to ourselves that we must consider other people's points of view, and be cognizant of other worlds, other circles overlapping with our own. That is Mary Garth's way, for example: look at how she thinks of her love for Fred. Fred has his own life to lead—and she insists that he lead it. She loves him, but she will not try to force him to live her way—nor will she give up her own way of life, her principles, to marry him.

Another way to overcome egotism is to suppress our desires, to be self-effacing. That is Mr. Farebrother's way, for example, in his helping Fred by speaking to Mary for him. Maybe such self-effacement, such repression of self, is not very healthy, however. Farebrother is in so many ways a defeated man: defeated by his vocation, by his circumstances, by his interests and inclinations, by his little self-indulgences, too. But he is not defeated by life; he can still serve others, as he serves Fred, with friendship.

A third way to overcome the limitations of egotism is to know the world largely: to "enlarge [our] sympathies." That is what Dorothea does, finally. She starts out, to be sure, wanting to outdo Farebrother at suppression of self—even before we meet Farebrother. But what happens through the course of the novel is that Dorothea learns more about the large world, understands it more, and can thus be more self-assertive in it.

When George Eliot was Dorothea's age, she wrote to her early friend and teacher, Maria Lewis, explaining her understanding of this idea: "The martyr at the stake seeks its gratification as much as the court sycophant, the difference lying in the comparative dignity and beauty of the two egos." While some people "talk absurdly of self-denial," she says, "to a being of moral excellence—the greatest torture . . . would be to run counter to the dictates of conscience."[59]

Self assertion is not the same thing as selfishness, nor is knowing one's self the same thing as being self-centered. Rosamond, for example, assumes—presumes—that she is the center of the world, and she sees no world other than her own. For the most part Lydgate operates the same way: he knows a much larger world than Rosamond knows, but he recognizes only one perspective on it—which is his own. Lydgate's knowledge of the world should remind him that it is a complex figure, but it does not; he insists on keeping it simple, and allows for only one center—again, his own—from which the world's meaning may radiate. Will recognizes the complexity of the world, and he knows that he must find something—some cause—to devote himself to in that world. He is also rather sure, however, that he is correct in his judgment of the world, and that he can organize its meaning to suit himself whenever he wants to. Dorothea, at the other extreme from Rosamond, is seeking access to the center of the world through someone else, or for access to someone else's center, for most of the novel. From Casaubon's death on, she begins to assert herself more in the world as she understands it, and to enlarge both her world and that understanding. She becomes more and more its center, too, by means of her understanding.

One of the mysteries of human existence is that of the relationship between center and circumference. Circles have fascinated us since we first became human—and maybe even before that. The wheel is important, not for transportation, but as the sign of our triumph over the idea of spatial limitation. You have to pick up a square lump or a cube, and move it from one place to another—or you push it, against the grain, across the floor. But a ball rolls: roundness careers along using its own form to make motion possible. And it travels without seeming to move.

Shelley says that poetry—art—is "at once the center and circumference of all thought."[60] The great reciprocal action that connects the phenomenal world to the inner world of meaning is that which moves between the real measure called circumference and that dimensionless idea called center. The action itself, by which the connection is made, is that radical thing called radius.

Dorothea does not presume to be the center of her world. But like Dickens's David Copperfield, who begins his novel questioning whether he is the "hero of [his] own life"[61] and proves in the end to be such, Dorothea ends up making the large world in some sense her own, and becoming its radiant, organizing center.

If we take as typical of Dorothea's attitude toward the world her determination to "do" something for Lydgate, to help him to "do what [he] meant to do" in life (529), we might take as typical of Rosamond's attitude her complaint to Lydgate, a few pages earlier, about his situation: she speaks not of his misery, or of wanting to "take any pains" for him as Dorothea did (526), or of wanting "to make other people's lives better to them" (528). Rosamond tells her husband, "Let us go to London. . . . Whatever misery I have to put up with, it will be easier away from here" (523). Dorothea's attitude is heroic and selfless: it takes her actively into a world of duty and value and meaning. Rosamond's attitude is cowardly and selfish: she wants to run away.

What she can "do" has been Dorothea's constant question, as she seeks to be useful to others. Rosamond asks only once what she can "do," and George Eliot tells us how she says it. In response to Lydgate's request for her help in matters concerning his debts, Rosamond asks, pettishly, "What can *I* do, Tertius?" George Eliot then says: "That little speech of four words, like so many others in all languages, is capable by varied vocal inflexions of expressing all states of mind from helpless dimness to exhaustive argumentative perception, from the completest self-devoting fellowship to the most neutral aloofness. Rosamond's thin utterance threw into the words What can *I* do! as much neutrality as they could hold" (410).

Dorothea, of course, has money—and Rosamond does not. George Eliot has made things much easier for Dorothea by freeing her from such practical worries as the paying of bills. We may want to acknowledge this advantage of Dorothea's before we judge Rosamond too harshly. The rich young lady who has jewels and easy access to other finery may take the noble way and reject such things as vulgar and valueless; but she who has not yet been familiar with the glut of privilege may desire a turn at fancy dress.

The first argument against this excuse for Rosamond's selfishness, of course, is Mary Garth. Another is that which pits Ladislaw against Lydgate. Will and Lydgate are both ambitious young men without fortunes of their own, and both have been brought this far in life by the assistance of elder relatives. Will has been supported by his cousin Casaubon, Lydgate by his uncle Sir Godwin. Oddly enough, they both have connections with actresses, too: Will's mother was "for the stage" (422), and Lydgate's first love was an actress (103). They both claim, too, to value their "personal independence" (323). As Lydgate raises this latter subject in conversation with Will, he means in fact financial independence, not some grand philosophical abstraction; he is thinking of how to deal with his debts. Egotistically, Lydgate believes that "a man may work for a special end with others whose motives and general course are equivocal, if he is quite sure of his personal independence, and that he is not working for his private interest—either pleasure or money" (323). He assumes that his own integrity—the "personal independence" of which he is "quite sure"—justifies his use of Bulstrode's money and influence as a means to achieve his end. Will's claim—"My personal independence is as important to me as yours is to you," he says—is that he is not interested in "money and place in the world."

Lydgate assumes his own importance, and expects to be paid handsomely for it. When his creditors repossess his furniture, he has to ask Bulstrode for money. Having "boasted . . . that he [is] totally independent of Bulstrode," Lydgate would rather "gamble" than ask Bulstrode for aid (465). But he goes to Bulstrode, and borrows a thousand pounds.

When Bulstrode attempts to give Will money, he refuses. Will is not willing to take "ill-gotten" money; his "unblemished honour is important" to him (431). Lydgate can "work . . . with others whose motives and general course are equivocal" (323), but Will cannot—because he values his honor even above his ambition.

Part of the reason Will is so concerned with his honor is his love for Dorothea, and his certainty that "it would have been impossible for him ever to tell [her] that he had accepted" Bulstrode's offer (432). To Will, Dorothea is a "perfect woman," a "presence" that inspires the best in him; he is her "worshipper" (300). Lydgate, "adoring" Rosamond, "rejects his work and runs up bills" (301); and Dorothea, to him, is worth two hundred pounds. Dorothea "is going to be splendid to our New Hospital," Lydgate says (302); to Will she is splendid all on her own, for who she is rather than for what she will do with her money.

The significance of these comparisons—Will's and Lydgate's responses to Dorothea, and Dorothea's and Rosamond's effects on Will and Lydgate—is the same, in terms of what we learn about Dorothea: because of her goodness, she causes good to happen. As these comparisons further define Will's and Lydgate's characters, they are revealing in another way: Will, we see, can be inspired, and has thus the potential for goodness; Lydgate, however, is unalterably himself—we need not expect anything good from him. Even when Dorothea relieves him of his debt to Bulstrode, and he appreciates her in his mind as someone like "the Virgin Mary," a woman whose "love might help a man more than her money," Lydgate still cannot change. Will fulfills himself, thanks to Dorothea; Lydgate's response to her is nil. He claims that Dorothea has "made a great difference in [his] courage by believing in [him]," but that difference is hard to find. She "believe[s]" that he has the "power to do great things," and urges him to "do what [he] meant to do" by "making [his] knowledge useful" (529); his response is pathetic in its self-pitying moral cowardice. "I must do as other men do," he says, "and think what will please the world and bring in money." She answers, "Now that is not brave" (530).

We have probably talked enough about Lydgate. But because

George Eliot keeps bringing us back to him—mercilessly, perhaps—
we must examine one final example of his failure. At the beginning of
chapter 45, George Eliot tells us that we must try to see things in
"different lights"—to learn, that is, by comparison. She then gives us
Middlemarch's version of Lydgate and his ideas about medicine, as a
contrast to what we heard in the previous chapter of his conception
of himself as a doctor. There Lydgate represented himself to Dorothea
as someone whose crime is "the offense of being young, and a new-
comer, and happening to know something more than the old inhabitants" (303). Here we get the other local doctors' points of view—the
views of those ignorant "old inhabitants." The cases they use to argue
against him are petty and mostly foolish: they are indeed ignorant
compared to Lydgate. But their sense of his character matches, largely,
with what we know about him already. Then George Eliot gives us
two long, detailed accounts of Lydgate's supposed professional successes. She might have given us cases like his successful treatment of
Fred's typhoid fever, which Mr. Wrench had not recognized—but she
does not. Instead, she relates comic cases of misunderstood success
that undercut the serious respect for him raised in us by the other
doctors' defensive ignorance. When Lydgate treats Mr. Trumbull's
pneumonia by simply watching him through his illness, the proud auc-
tioneer—flattered into thinking that together they have advanced
medical science—endorses Lydgate for "knowing a thing or two more
than the rest of the doctors" (312). When Mrs. Larcher's maid comes
to Lydgate with what Dr. Minchin has diagnosed as "tumor," Lydgate
is able to dissolve it, miraculously, because it is in reality only a
cramped muscle—but his treatment of "this amazing case" becomes
"the proof of his marvellous skill" (311).

It is in the context of these great medical successes of Lydgate's
that George Eliot gives us a brief scene between him and his Rosamond. He lies on a sofa, an "emotional elephant," indulging in daydreams of his own greatness. "I am thinking," he tells his wife, "of a
great fellow, who was about as old as I am, three hundred years ago,
and had already begun a new era in anatomy" (315). Thinking com-

paratively, he puts himself in Vesalius's place, for like Vesalius, he too has "enemies": "No wonder the medical fogies in Middlemarch are jealous, when some of the greatest doctors living were fierce upon Vesalius" (316). But Rosamond is bored by Lydgate's self-laudatory dreams and ambitions; she doesn't like medicine as a profession, and says she does not like being married to a medical man. He objects— "Don't say that again, dear, it pains me"—but he surrenders to her, "giving up remonstrance and petting her resignedly" (316).

Lydgate's failure is a failure of will. He has not the will to be an extraordinary man—like Vesalius. And George Eliot criticizes him not just for the proud vanity of his daydreaming, but for the ease with which he abandons his dreams, to pet Rosamond. Lydgate wants "to do worthy" things, and he tells Rosamond, "A man must work to do that, my pet"; but then he admits that he is "too entirely contented" with his "pet" to "make discoveries," and he sets aside will and work for pleasure.

Dante's *Purgatorio* contains an important discussion of "free will," and a lovely image for how it works. We are attracted to pleasure, Dante says, by our passions. Desire moves us toward it. Then intellect, following desire, examines the pleasure, and if it approves bends in sympathy with desire. That union—the agreement of intellect with passion—is what Dante calls "free will."[62] It is what George Eliot calls thought and feeling, acting together. Lydgate turns off thought, when feeling strikes his fancy—and thus he is not free. For all of his boasts of independence, he has no free will.

Will is an odd word for this novel, a double pun associating free will, and Will Ladislaw, and Casaubon's will. All three converge in Book 5. George Eliot examines both Lydgate and Will himself as characters who pretend to exercise free will, and with the intrusion of Casaubon's will introduces the fundamental test of Dorothea's freedom.

Dorothea's freedom poses a terrible threat to Casaubon's ego, and Will Ladislaw threatens his masculinity. Will goes to church at Lowick one bright spring morning in order to see Dorothea there: he decides to go, George Eliot says, by accepting the passionate voice of "Inclination" over the intelligent voice of "Objection" (326). His visit is a complete failure, however, as he knew—intelligently—it would be. Casaubon is furious at Will's appearance there, and leads Dorothea away without acknowledging Will's presence. The pretty spring day disappears for Will as he walks back to Middlemarch: "the lights . . . all changed for him both within and without" (328).

At home at Lowick, Dorothea feels herself "in a virtual tomb" (329). That evening she begins her new "sifting" work with her husband. In the middle of the night Dorothea awakens, and finds him up. She reads to him. His mind is alert, and he interrupts her, saying "That will do—mark that," or "Pass on to the next head." One section that he tells her to "omit" is "the second excursus on Crete" (330). This may be just a specific example of "pass[ing] on to the next head," but it may also contain an interesting irony. For the mythographer, Crete is the source of the story of Pasiphaë, the wife of King Minos, who became enamored of a great bull, coupled with it, and gave birth to the Minotaur. That story could be too threatening for Casaubon to have Dorothea read to him in the middle of the night; he may also prefer not to hear about the labyrinth in which Minos imprisoned his wife's Minotaur either.

When the reading finally ends, the lights are again extinguished, and husband and wife go back to bed. Lying in the dark, then, Casaubon makes his request for Dorothea's blind promise to abide by his wishes after his death. He knows what he wants—he has already executed his shameful will. He not only wants to bind Dorothea to his work, to living out her life in his scholarly "tomb"; he also wants to bind her away from contact with masculine life or sex—away from Ladislaw. He would bind her to his will, and away from her own, and away from Will.

Brooke tries to explain Casaubon's dislike for Will as the result of their academic disagreements, and he burbles out "Thoth and Dagon" (335) as somehow examples of what he means. Ironically he blunders upon exactly the right explanation for Casaubon's fear of Will: Thoth was an Egyptian god of wisdom, Dagon a Philistine god of fertility.

Once Casaubon is dead, Dorothea begins to "exert" herself (338) at Lowick, eagerly assuming the "duties" of ownership (342). She is constrained by Casaubon's will, however, in regard to her natural inclinations toward Ladislaw. She feels "indignation" at his making it at least ethically impossible for her to give Will half of her property; but otherwise she is free. One of the items on her list of duties is the "living" at Lowick, which is now hers "to give away" (340). Lydgate recommends Farebrother to her. Farebrother is an excellent preacher, a "remarkable fellow" whose "plain, easy eloquence" lets people listen to him (342).

Lydgate also knows the Reverend Mr. Tyke, and, in recommending Farebrother to Dorothea as "one of the most blameless men," Lydgate is "making amends for the casting-vote he had once given with an ill-satisfied conscience" (342). Dorothea and Lydgate discuss Farebrother's and Tyke's different styles of preaching and compare them in terms of their suitability for the parishioners at Lowick. Because Lydgate has called Farebrother a "blameless" man, and because the living to be bestowed is Casaubon's, perhaps the comparison we should be more interested in making is that between the "blameless" man and Casaubon himself. When we think of Casaubon, at this point in the novel, we must think of his will—and blame him for that.

Thinking of Farebrother's "plain, easy eloquence" maybe we also look ahead to poor Brooke, in the next chapter of Book 5, trying to make a speech. George Eliot's point in inviting us to make such a comparison is not merely to deride Brooke for his incompetence; it is more than that. It places two parallel forms of service to humanity side by side, for a moment, for analysis. Both the living at Lowick and a seat in Parliament must be filled.

Dorothea questions whether Tyke's "pinching" doctrines and his arguments "about imputed righteousness and the prophecies in the Apocalypse" are of any service to humanity. She thinks not; she is looking for a Christianity "that makes . . . a wide blessing . . . takes in the most good of all kinds, and brings in the most people as sharers in it" (343).

Brooke's attempt at politics serves nobody. He is unwilling to take a stand on anything, and unable to speak. He is mocked and derided for his feeble and silly attempt to serve humanity.

Dorothea eventually chooses Farebrother over Tyke for the parish at Lowick—and George Eliot chooses Will over Brooke for a career in politics. Will is not ready to stand for Parliament yet, but he starts now to "dream of wonders that he might do" in "political writing, political speaking" (351). But the comparison implied here is not a true one. Farebrother preaches "eloquent" sermons every week and will do so whether he gets the living at Lowick or not: his goodness as a preacher is not a means to some other or greater end. Will's political ambition, however, is not to serve the people so much as it is to serve himself: he wants to win "such distinction" (351) that he can return to Middlemarch and marry Dorothea.

The next scene in the novel invites us to compare both Will's ambition for himself—his will—and Casaubon's last will to the way Farebrother acts. The "eloquent" man intervenes to talk with Mary, for Fred. His intervention is against what he could well argue as his own best interests. But he does not argue that; rather, he does what he thinks is right, despite his own desires. In George Eliot's words for Dorothea's later act of heroic generosity, Farebrother is able to "clutch [his] own pain, and compel it to silence, and think of" Fred and Mary (544).

Farebrother's selflessness contrasts with Will's selfishness or self-centeredness. But we can sympathize with Will's dream: he is not planning not to work, or—like Lydgate—abandoning his work for his pleasure. He wants to do good things in politics in order to win the right to marry Dorothea, whom he loves. It is not a selfless ambition, and maybe it does not qualify as an ambition of free will; but at least his "young dream" is not altogether corrupt or bad.

When we compare Casaubon's will with Farebrother's act, however, we come to a different conclusion. Casaubon was unwilling to give up Dorothea, even in death. Farebrother gives up Mary—even in life: Casaubon the pedant seemed to be a passionless man, and Mrs. Cadwallader had a dozen funny things to say about his painfully passionless self. But Mrs. Cadwallader was wrong, and so were we: Casaubon *is* a passionate man. He is, at the last, a violently passionate man. Both in his horrible request to Dorothea and in his last will he is shamefully limited by passion. He is not free. He does not know how to love. His will is enslaved by a passionate selfishness, by jealousy and greed.

Casaubon's is the second testamentary bequest read into the novel, and much the worse of the two. Peter Featherstone, a mean and ungenerous man in life, gave away his money when he died. He had to: we all have to give away our things when we die. But Casaubon, petty and passionately selfish, won't—can't—give up his own will when he dies.

Lydgate surrenders his will—for greatness, for accomplishment—to Rosamond. Farebrother, in his generosity, gives up his will—his desire for Mary—to help make both Fred and Mary happy. Dorothea tries to give up Will Ladislaw for Casaubon, and tries to give up both her volitional will and Ladislaw in order to "save" Rosamond (545); finally she relinquishes her fortune to act by free will, and marries Will Ladislaw because she loves him. But Casaubon? He is neither a wise man nor a free man. He dies, a victim of his pathetic passion. And his death is horrible, compared to old Peter Featherstone's.

Casaubon's life was horrible, too. What made it so was his selfishness, mostly. Farebrother's life is a good one—not because of his great collection of beetles, or because he finally succeeds to the living at Lowick church and can relax at whist. His life is good because he acts for the good, socially. His act in speaking to Mary is a simple good thing—and it accomplishes good. It works as well—as effectively, as substantially—as Caleb Garth's estate management techniques or agricultural efficiencies and reforms.

Casaubon accomplished nothing in his life: nothing as a scholar, nothing as a husband, nothing—it seems—as a minister. Farebrother, however, is a good scientist: he has "made an exhaustive study of the entomology of [the] district," and is confident that he has "done [his] insects well" (118). He has not married "because," as Lydgate tells

Dorothea, "his mother, aunt, and sister all live with him, and depend on him" (342). He has made a significant local reputation for himself by the quality of his weekly sermons. Farebrother serves others with his life, and he does this as a scholar, a family man, and a priest. Casaubon serves no one—not even himself.

Though Casaubon is in no way a religious man—despite his being the Reverend Mr. Casaubon—his counterpart in the novel, Nicholas Bulstrode, pretends piously to do God's work. George Eliot contrasts Farebrother's behavior with what Bulstrode does, and with Bulstrode's selfish exercise of his will. Bulstrode is an offensive man from the first time he is mentioned. He is a banker who "dislike[s] coarseness and profanity" (60). Peter Featherstone calls him, ironically, "a fine, religious, charitable" man, a "speckilating fellow" who "may come down any day, when the devil leaves off backing him" (75). In describing him—"he had a pale blond skin, thin grey-besprinkled hair, light-grey eyes, and a large forehead"—George Eliot says nothing particularly negative; but she makes his tone of voice "inconsistent with openness," and gives him a "deferential bending attitude in listening" that seems false. The most acute observers in Middlemarch, she says, want to know "who his father and grandfather were" (83).

At the end of Book 5, George Eliot exposes Bulstrode's past. We have long since come to agree with those of his critics who call him a "Pharisee" (83); now we find out, not about his father and grandfather, but more importantly how he came to be the rich banker he is today. The device that George Eliot uses to introduce Bulstrode's past is clumsily plotty and arbitrary, certainly. John Raffles has no purpose in the novel except as a carrier of Bulstrode's past and a threat to his present and future. But that past is important enough for the whole of the novel for us to excuse the manner of its introduction.

The individual parts of *Middlemarch*—its eight books—are very carefully organized units. They are works of art, one after another. Their form, individually, tells us something more about how George Eliot works. Book 5 begins with Dorothea's seeking information from Lydgate about her husband's health, because she wants to help him as much as she can. It includes Dorothea's determination to do something for Middlemarch, and to help Lydgate with the hospital, and Farebrother's aid to Fred in talking to Mary. It also includes Casaubon's attempt to hurt both Dorothea and Will, and concludes with Raffles teasing Bulstrode with the information he has, threatening to destroy him.

The title of Book 5, "The Dead Hand," refers to Casaubon's hand and its outrageously intended weight upon the living present, to banish Ladislaw. When Bulstrode has to deal with Raffles at the end of the book, his first interest is to banish Raffles. He fails at that, and the last we hear is Raffles's exclamation upon his discovery of Will's name. At first Raffles is to Bulstrode as Will is to Casaubon. Then Raffles connects Will to Bulstrode, and suddenly past, present, and future are balanced, and all the themes of the novel are set to converge with Will, now, at their center.

Reform, freedom, the relationship between thought and feeling, art and sympathy, love: all of those concepts are concerned with how we use what we know. The elements of plot that entangle Bulstrode, Raffles, and then Lydgate are involved with this question in a negative way. To understand positively, affirmatively, how we must use what we know, we have to look to Will—and Dorothea.

Dorothea and Will both learn how to use what they know. It brings them together, first, as they admit that they love each other. Beyond that afternoon they use what they know for us, and for our world. All the various themes of *Middlemarch* lead toward this kind of life. For George Eliot, both art and life are—at their best and fullest—"mode[s] of amplifying experience and extending our contact with our fellow men beyond the bounds of our personal lot."[63]

· 11 ·

RELATIONSHIPS

With the exception of "Miss Brooke" the titles of the eight books of *Middlemarch* all identify their subjects in terms of thematic matters rather than character. Most of them propose to consider their themes through some form of comparative focus: Book 2 is "Old and Young," Book 4 "Three Love Problems," Book 6 "The Widow and the Wife," Book 7 "Two Temptations," Book 8 "Sunrise and Sunset."

The eponymous characters in "The Widow and the Wife" are Dorothea, as the widow, and Rosamond, as the wife. The book begins and ends with Dorothea, in scenes with Will; Rosamond appears in two chapters in the middle, once with Lydgate and the other time with Will. The rest of the book is taken up with other situations and relationships which we see first in themselves and then in comparison to the idea or theme which George Eliot creates by contrasting the widow and the wife.

Situations, by themselves, are no more important than plot; they are, in fact, what plot is made of. But plot is not interesting in a novel or elsewhere. Plot has no meaning. People who talk about plot—who tell stories as plot—do not know how to talk about meaning, and they reduce life to something like a trip-ticket from an automobile club. "My Trip to Minneapolis" becomes a dull, stupid tale: you take I-94 all the way, except for the route around Chicago on the Illinois Turnpike.

To tell plot and call it life is like writing an autobiography simply recording age. "First I was one, and then two, and then three. . . . I was six, and after that seven. Soon I was eight and nine, and before long ten. Another twelve months and I was eleven. That year passed, and I was twelve." In the second volume there's a dramatic and even rhetorical build-up all through the teens—thirteen, fourteen, fifteen, sixteen, seventeen, eighteen, nineteen—and then, climactically, twenty. And twenty-one. Interest in plot alone is a sign of an inadequate response to human existence. As I suggested earlier, we should perhaps forgive plottiness in a work of art if what the artist achieves as meaning is truly great.

The main plottiness of *Middlemarch* comes in Books 5 and 6, with Raffles having to give us all the previously unknown history of Will's family. When Lydgate was introduced, George Eliot stopped to tell us all about him, "to make the new settler . . . better known to anyone interested in him than he could possibly be even to those . . . in Middlemarch" (96). Will, however, does not know his own past; nobody knows it until Raffles comes along. The importance of its discovery derives from how Will responds to the situation his new knowledge puts him in. George Eliot gave us Lydgate's past so that we could better understand his present character; much later in the novel she gives us Will's past not for what it says about Will, but for what his response to learning it means for the novel. Situation makes meaning possible; it gives character something to learn, and thus enables meaning.

The occasion for Will's learning his past comes at a furniture auction. Bulstrode has commissioned Will to buy a painting for Mrs. Bulstrode. "The Supper at Emmaus" is the painting; its subject should be, appropriately, who one's friends are. Raffles is at the auction, hears Will's name, and recognizes him. Before Will can escape, Raffles has told him about his mother, and why she ran away from her family.

Will's first response to what he hears is to feel "as if he had dirt cast upon him amidst shouts of scorn" (422). He is ashamed of his past because of what "Dorothea's friends" will think if they hear it. He knows that he has nothing to be ashamed of—"let them suspect what they pleased, they would find themselves in the wrong" (423)—but still he is ashamed.

The important relation that George Eliot gives us as a focus is not Will's with his mother or his mother's family, or his relation with "Dorothea's friends." The important relation for Will—which he can't see—is his relation with Dorothea. Distracted by social insignificances and irrelevant details, he loses sight of his love for her. If Will could only think more clearly about what he has just learned, he would beat down his shame, accept his past, and dismiss Raffles—and his plot.

Dorothea knows that her relation with Will is important to her, but she has her own difficulty in understanding what that importance is. At the beginning of Book 6, Dorothea buries Casaubon for a second time by writing her note to him, refusing "to submit [her] soul to [his]." Immediately, then, she thinks of Will, "longing . . . to see" him (372). Though "her soul thirst[s] to see him," she doesn't think of loving him, or being in love. She only thinks of giving him some-thing—which she cannot do, because of that shameful item in her own past, Casaubon's will. But Dorothea knows—if she stops to think—that she does not value material wealth, so she should not be con-cerned about giving it up or about giving it to Will.

Dorothea writes the dead Casaubon that note of final denial for her soul's sake. The note asserts her independence from his life both past and future. She does not yet think of a future with Ladislaw, but she does think of and toward the future. She would like to help Will toward his future, and she wants to do something with her own.

As for the past, Dorothea honors what Will has meant to her, as inspiration to her soul, and she wants to see him—begins even to look for him, to seek him both at Farebrother's house and at Lowick church. George Eliot approves: "Life would be no better than candlelight tinsel and daylight rubbish if our spirits were not touched by what has been, to tissues of longing and constancy" (372).

Dorothea and Will have two scenes together in Book 6, both unsatisfactory to them as well as to us. On both occasions Dorothea tries to focus her interest in Will on her desire to give him money, because she is forbidden to give him love. What we see, as readers, is that Dorothea is not so independent as she would like to be. Despite her formal and symbolic dismissal of him, Casaubon still controls her future, just as meanly as he intended to.

Will has always claimed freedom and independence—but in these two scenes with Dorothea he is as harnessed as Lydgate ever is. Will's harness, however, is not—like Lydgate's—one he has submitted to; Will's yoke is one he has fashioned for himself, out of pride. He wants Dorothea to love him and to acknowledge as much. In his pride and anger at his situation, he cannot speak openly or respond freely to what she says. In their first scene, in chapter 54, Will informs Dorothea that he is going away, "to begin a new life" (371). Though he announces this departure as his own plan, Will is irritated that Dorothea may "approve of [his] going away for years" and not coming back to Middlemarch until he has made his "mark in the world" (375). "I shall never hear from you," he says, in angry self-pity; "And you will forget all about me." Dorothea replies, easily and earnestly, "I shall never forget you." Hearing this, Will should be free to speak to her, to tell her his love. But his pride controls him; he "look[s] almost angry," and rejects the possibility of any sort of "confession" of love (375). Instead of feeling for Dorothea, Will is full of "petulance." They conclude their interview awkwardly and unhappily.

Their second scene together is no better. This time Dorothea asks Will to "remember" her, and he responds "Why should you say that? . . . as if I were not in danger of forgetting everything else" (438). But he says this "with irritation" and with "a movement of anger against her." She feels "joy . . . that it was really herself whom Will loved"— but her joy is sadly limited: his leaving, she assumes, means his "renouncing" that love, out of "honour" (438). Moments later, Dorothea passes Will in her carriage; he is walking away from Lowick. She could stop for him, but she doesn't; "leaving him behind," unable to "look back at him," she feels "as if a crowd of indifferent objects had thrust them asunder . . . taking them farther and farther away from each other, and making it useless to look back" (439).

On its own, the furniture auction at which Will meets Raffles and learns of his past has little enough to do with the meaning of the novel, though George Eliot spends three pages or so describing it. Mr. Larcher's possessions are to be auctioned, not because of his failure, but because of the kind of "success" which requires him to move up in the world: he has bought a successful doctor's house. George Eliot crosses this "festival" occasion with Doctor Lydgate's having to explain to Rosamond that he has used their furniture as security to renew one of his loans. Offended at the idea of a "man" coming "to make an inventory of the furniture" (410), Rosamond proposes that they simply "leave Middlemarch" instead—and have, like Larcher, a regular "sale" (410). They disagree, and Rosamond reflects pettishly that "if she had known how Lydgate would behave, she would never have married him" (412). Lydgate, for his part, tries to forget their disagreement, tries to hide—at least momentarily—from this problem: "Come, darling, let us make the best of things. . . . Kiss me" (413).

Like Will, Lydgate has a family. But Lydgate's is an asset—or is supposed to be one. He has an uncle who is a baronet, and Rosamond is certain Sir Godwin will solve his nephew's financial problems for him, particularly since that nephew is married to a gorgeous and attractive woman. When the baronet's third son, a somewhat dashing captain in uniform, comes to visit, Rosamond is much taken with him and justifies her attentions to him in part as something like good business. Against Lydgate's wishes—contrary, in fact, to his instructions as a doctor—a pregnant Rosamond decides to go horseback riding with Captain Lydgate. She pays no attention to Lydgate's warning, despite his claim that he is "the person to judge for" her, at least in medical matters. Lydgate cannot object to her ignoring his warning or command; he is "resigned." Rosamond will not agree with him, or even smile for him—but he is still her slave. Rather than argue with her he lies to himself, and accepts "the lovely curves of her face" as "good tempered enough without [her] smiling" (402). The result of his weakness and Rosamond's selfishness is that she has a miscarriage—and Lydgate loses his "family."

After Fred accidentally gets himself a situation as Caleb Garth's assistant, he decides to go tell Mary. He is going to be gainfully and even usefully employed now; even if the employment does mean that he will have "gone down a step in life" (392), it is work that will make Fred respectable in Mary's eyes—or should. He stops first to speak to Mrs. Garth, who is not as generous as her husband in her regard for Fred. Susan knows that Fred will be "trouble" to Caleb, and resents his taking Fred on to work with him. She resents even more Fred's hope of marrying Mary someday. By the time Susan has finished talking with Fred she has said more than she had intended to say, and he leaves her feeling the uncomfortable beginnings of jealousy for Farebrother as his "rival" (398).

Farebrother, of course, is determined in his honesty not to be Fred's rival in any way. When Fred speaks to Mary, however, he is "piqued," and there is "rage in his tone." He accuses Mary, not of preferring Farebrother, but of being wise enough to do so: "When you are constantly seeing a man who beats me at everything," he complains, "I can have no fair chance" (399).

Dorothea's and Will's two scenes together in Book 6 are painful, moving, potentially tragic. They do not yet know how to love each other, and at the end of their second scene, at the conclusion of the book, they part. Will's "pride" is "a repellant force, keeping him asunder from Dorothea" (377); her failure to "do as [she] liked" (376)— and to admit that what she likes is love—keeps them apart as well. Because they fail to act positively toward each other in this situation, they are "forced . . . along different paths, taking them farther and farther away from each other" (439).

Lydgate's and Rosamond's scene in Book 6—Rosamond's "wife" scene—is like any other scene between them in its first meaning: it demonstrates, again, that they do not love each other, and that neither of them even knows what love is. This scene is perhaps more pathetic than most of theirs because it is set in the context of Rosamond's miscarriage, at the beginning, and ends with Lydgate's utter surrender to her.

Fred's and Mary's scene is different from either of these others. He and Mary are not tragic characters, nor are they pathetic. When we compare their story with the other two, theirs becomes the stuff of simple life, a comic affirmation of the possibility of human happiness. Without the intrusion of scientific advance, political reform, religion, or even ardor and planning—and in spite of all our errors at gambling or otherwise—Fred and Mary assure us with welcome evidence that there is some sort of good ordained and determined for this poor world.

When Fred turns "sulkily" away from Mary, pouting jealously at being "bowled out by Farebrother," Mary feels an "inclination to laugh" at him. She calls him "delightfully ridiculous," her own "charming simpleton." Still unsure of the situation and its significance, Fred asks, boyishly, "Do you really like me best, Mary?" (400). Fred, we know, has "always loved" Mary since they were children. Fred is no longer a child, but he is still growing up and on the verge of falling in love as an adult. And Mary, though seemingly always an adult, makes a new kind of resolution as well; when she agrees "to herself" to accept Fred as her serious, grown-up lover, she allows herself a "smile" of pleasure at the happy choice (400).

Fred's and Mary's relationship is much more central to the meaning of *Middlemarch* than their situation is to the plot. Mary seems to have no situation, almost: she stays with old Peter Featherstone, she stays at home, she stays with Farebrother and his family, she comes back home again. Fred has or is involved in a number of situations: he doesn't get an inheritance, he does not—and then does—get his degree from Cambridge, he fails to pay his debts, he gets sick. But his situations are of no significance; they do not cause anything more to happen than Mary's undramatic life does. Fred and Mary are important, however, to each other: and because of the relationship between them—because they are in love, or are learning to be in love—they are important to *Middlemarch*.

Relations are important in life: relations, not substances or situations. Though *Middlemarch* is packed with things and people, with situations and information, actions and facts and an elaborately complicated plot, its meaning grows out of the relationships—or refusals of relationships—which it develops. The novel is not "Miss Brooke"— could never have been so, I suspect: from the moment of her creation on, Dorothea seems to have been in need of a world to join, to bind her life to.

The novel begins by showing us Dorothea in relation to Celia, who is in fact her "relation," her sister. They discuss their dead mother's jewels, and at the end of the first chapter are ready for "going into society" (7). Before long we meet Peter Featherstone, and his many relations; and we see his determination to exclude them all, to thwart their greedy familial expectations and deny—in effect—any relationship with them. Instead he claims, in death, a previously unknown and unacknowledged relation, Joshua Rigg. And Rigg, having adopted his father's name in order to qualify for his inheritance, sells the Farebrother estate as soon as he gets it, and leaves the novel.

Casaubon and Will are related, as cousins. Casaubon acknowledges this in the smallest way, by providing Will with money; he rejects any form of human relationship with him. Casaubon and Dorothea are related, as husband and wife—but he rejects her attempts to make marriage a serious relationship. Other than these two, Casaubon has no relations; he lives alone, and dies of "fatty degeneration of the heart" (292–93).

Sir James loves Dorothea, early on in the novel, but she refuses such a relationship with him—so he marries Celia. He still thinks of Dorothea as a "queen," however, and builds her model cottages on his estate. Unlike Brooke, who hardly knows that his tenant farmers exist, Sir James cares for them, and believes that he is "bound to do the best" for them (263).

Relationships

Ned Plymdale enters the novel as a young man who wants to marry Rosamond; but she will have none of him, so he is dismissed and quickly disappears. Lydgate and Rosamond marry—but Lydgate doesn't understand what a relationship should be, and Rosamond rejects the idea of such. To Rosamond, a husband has material value; if that husband has an uncle who is a baronet he is all the more valuable.

Lydgate and Bulstrode are "related," in their project at the fever hospital, though Lydgate claims to be "independent" of the banker who finances his work. Despite Lydgate's claim, Bulstrode uses their relationship to his advantage.

Bulstrode and Will are related, by marriage. Bulstrode would rather not have known of such a connection, but knowing it—and afraid—he acknowledges it to Will. Will rejects their relationship, and refuses the money which Bulstrode tries to give him. Bulstrode and Raffles have an old business connection, a relationship that Bulstrode wants desperately to hide. Caleb Garth discovers it—and what it means—and breaks his own business connection with Bulstrode. Bulstrode then tries to buy Raffles's silence; failing at that, he uses his relationship with Lydgate to buy his doctor's silence, in effect, and manages to close Raffle's mouth forever.

Fred has a financial relationship with Caleb, which he breaks. He has a sort of relationship with his uncle Peter Featherstone, or at least thinks he does; but he is frustrated—like the rest of Featherstone's relatives—and gets nothing for his troubles. We first see Fred's relationship with Mary when she is taking care of Featherstone, at Stone Lodge; she will not encourage Fred—will not let the relationship between them become a serious one—because he is not yet worthy of such. When Fred wants to talk to her about their relationship and his worth, he asks Farebrother to help him, depending on Farebrother's relation to them both as a mutual friend. When Fred needs more than a friend—when he needs a teacher, a guide, a father—he turns to Caleb again, and Caleb offers him just that relationship.

Mr. Vincy, upset at his son's relation with Garth, at first would "wash [his] hands of" Fred (392); he relents, however, and only complains to his wife, "We must expect to have trouble with our children" (393). Vincy's sister is married to Bulstrode, so the Vincys and the Bulstrodes are related—but neither of the men likes the idea.

From the beginning Vincy opposes his daughter's marriage to Lydgate; when Rosamond applies to her father for money, he refuses her request. She then writes to Lydgate's uncle, trying to use that relationship to get money. Sir Godwin writes back to break the connection altogether: he tells his nephew, "you must consider yourself on your own legs entirely now" (459).

Three of the six principle young people in *Middlemarch* are orphans. Because of that, the relationships they enter into are all the more important. Sir Godwin was Lydgate's guardian when he was a boy; his only other uncle "has had a grudge against" him (459). Casaubon is Will's only blood relation. Dorothea has her sister and her uncle Brooke. Otherwise, these three characters all have to make their own relationships in this world.

We have already examined Lydgate's relations, all of which fail. The last we hear of him is his having told Rosamond, before his death, that she has been his "basil plant," the relation being "that basil was a plant which . . . flourished wonderfully on a murdered man's brains" (575). If relationship is what is valuable in life—and it is, certainly, for the artist who would "enlarge men's sympathies"—then Lydgate's life has in the end no value. He has made money, finally, but that is all; "he [has] not done what he once meant to do." He has accomplished neither "good things" nor "great things," and his marriage does not compensate for his surrender of purpose. He "regard[s] himself as a failure" (575).

Will's relationships throughout the novel are troublesome. Casaubon supports him, but does so grudgingly—and Will responds in kind. Casaubon had once intended Will to be his secretary, but Will "turned out to be—not good enough" (251) to satisfy in such a relationship. Will is "self-indulgent" (55), and his insistence on doing as he likes (376) makes relations with others difficult. One of the disturbing "irregularities" of his self-indulgent character, as far as Middlemarch is concerned, is his tendency to "stretch himself out at length on the rug" in Middlemarch parlors. Such "oddity" seems almost antisocial to properly civilized people.

Will works with Brooke as secretary, speech-writer, and editor, but does not like the way this "relation" (322) proceeds, and he feels "harnessed" (324) by it and unhappy. He and Rosamond seem to have a sort of relationship, but in fact simply use each other. Will finds Lydgate's house comfortable—there are no restrictions there about lying on the rug—and Rosamond diverting. He amuses himself with her, singing and talking in his old "dilettanteish" way. He is not particularly kind to Rosamond—"he pouted, and was wayward . . . often uncomplimentary"—but becomes "necessary to her entertainment by his companionship in her music, his varied talk, and his freedom from [Lydgate's] grave preoccupation" (321).

Raffles claims a relation with Ladislaw because he knows Will's history, but Will rejects the claim. Bulstrode, however, cannot so easily reject Raffles; what Raffles knows about Bulstrode is incriminating. In an attempt to preempt Raffles's blackmail, Bulstrode tries to "make amends" to Will—but is rebuffed. Though Will is "without fortune" (430) and is very conscious of needing one, he values his "unblemished honour" (431) more than money and rejects Bulstrode's offer. If he could, he would deny any form of relationship with Bulstrode: "If I had a fortune of my own," he says, "I would be willing to pay it to any one who could disprove what you have told me" (431).

Will does not submit to relationships easily. His one seriousness, for most of the novel, may be his notion of his "personal independence" (323). Will's independence, however, means doing what he wants to do more than anything grandly ethical or philosophical. The relationships he is most comfortable with in Middlemarch are those that let him indulge himself in play. He enjoys taking Henrietta Noble on his arm "in the eyes of the town"—and his enjoyment with her is exactly like that which he gets from his relationship with the "troop of droll children" whom he entertains with "excursions" and "a small feast of gingerbread" (320). Were we to give a name to Will's behavior in all of these various social relations we might be tempted to call him an adolescent. But Will is awkwardly old for adolescence: he is twenty-three or twenty-four by Book 6. He needs to grow up.

At the beginning of the novel Dorothea's insistence on living a noble life also has something of adolescence to it. But the adolescence there is Dorothea's flaw, not her ambition's. She is naive, but her ambition is not. Her ambition is one we should all have—and one which perhaps we all did have, at some point in our adolescence. Most of us abandon our ideals, however, and say—self-deceptively—that we have outgrown them.

Dorothea is a serious young woman who intends to do good and live a useful life. Her seriousness has already enabled her to set up "an infant school . . . in the village" (4), and though we do not hear of her taking children on picnics, we know that she supervises goings on at her school and that she visits tenant farmers and their families, to try to help them. She wants to be related to the world and has little time—in principle—for lesser ambitions.

Dorothea and Celia are very different people, for all that they are sisters. They are related, however, and they both value being so. Celia frequently does not understand Dorothea and often assumes that because Dorothea is not acting as Celia would act—or as people in general should act—she must be wrong. Dorothea is wiser than Celia, and from the beginning she understands their relationship better. She knows her sister and knows how the two of them are different. Dorothea often disagrees with Celia, and sometimes condescends to her; but she does not try to make Celia into someone she is not.

Dorothea has been raised in part at Brooke's home; he is her guardian. But he lacks the intelligence, the sensitivity, and the seriousness to guard or guide Dorothea. Their relationship is one of familial piety for the most part. Even when Dorothea is being immature, or making mistakes—big mistakes, like marrying Casaubon—she is more mature and more responsible than her uncle.

I have discussed at length Dorothea's marriage relationship with Casaubon. The only thing that may still need to be said about it is

that Dorothea learns a great deal from her attempt to be his wife. She
learns better judgment; though she will never be a skeptic, she does
learn to examine things more closely before she acts or judges. She
also learns to see herself better. That does not mean that she becomes
self-centered, but that she becomes self-aware and can consider her
position in various situations with more justice. And seeing a man so
small, so limited as eventually she recognizes Casaubon to be, Dorothea learns to want a much larger life than she ever considered before.
Because of what she has learned from her marriage about smallness
and limitation, she wants now to know the world. And because her
marriage has taught her what love is not, she is ready—almost—to
learn what love is.

Dorothea's marriage to Casaubon is not a relationship at all.
From the beginning Dorothea mis-sees him: she cannot see either the
"two white moles" on his face (9) or that he is a "dried bookworm"
(11). She misreads his letter to her, thinking it is a love letter (29). And
almost as soon as they are married, Casaubon discovers his mistake
in taking a wife and withdraws from everything except the formalities
of a marriage relationship.

Perhaps what we most expect from—and for—Dorothea after
Casaubon's death is that she will now find a genuine relationship with
someone worthy of her, and that she will learn true love. For many
readers of *Middlemarch* Will is not someone worthy of Dorothea;
these readers share to the end Sir James's objection "that she ought
not to have married Ladislaw" (576). And numbers of Dorothea's critics agree with those "who knew her" that it is "a pity that so substan-
tive and rare a creature should have been absorbed into the life of
another, and be only known in a certain circle as a wife and mother"
(576). Such readers seem to me to need to look beyond their "certain
circle." They seem, too, to ignore Will's importance to Dorothea and
to her learning, as well as Will's own growth toward serious purpose.
Most important, they ignore the basically wonderful fact of love.

Relationships are difficult. They require a great deal of us. All too
often life is a series of missed relationships, or failed relationships.

Without relationships life has only plot—and mileage markers along the interstate, between Ann Arbor and Minneapolis. Sure, it has exit signs, entrance ramps, and traffic as you near Chicago, but that's not enough—for life!

George Eliot is not just being old-fashioned or conservative in having her heroine fall in love and marry. George Eliot, remember, was not legally married to the Victorian gentleman whom she called her husband for nearly twenty-five years. She neither idealized nor sentimentalized marriage in her life or in her fiction.

A lot of people misread the end of *Middlemarch* the same way they misread Jane Austen's novels. To them, Jane Austen wrote novels about that horrible time nearly two hundred years ago when young women were obliged to marry in order to have any kind of decent lives. That is nonsense, of course. Jane Austen certainly never idealizes marriage: her novels are full of disastrous marriages and failed marriages of all sorts. Usually, in a Jane Austen novel, there will be a young woman—the heroine—who will manage to create a genuine relationship with a man. Usually, then, the two of them will marry. Their marriage gives us hope—not because marriage symbolizes relationship; that is unnecessary, since we already have the relationship itself. Rather, their marriage gives us hope because two people, seriously related, may save the idea of marriage. They may make marriage—that social convention for lovers and friends—work again.

At the end of *Middlemarch* George Eliot presents the same kind of argument to us. And it is an argument: "to argue" means to make clear, to enlighten. It comes from the Latin verb *arguo,* and from Greek and Sanskrit words meaning brightness, and shining.

The end of *Middlemarch* seems to me gloriously bright and shining—even though the last image of the novel is that of "unvisited tombs." In the final pages George Eliot settles all the relationships we have been looking at, and then—at the very end—talks about the novel's relationship to us. Art's relation to life takes us all the way back to Rome, to Dorothea and Will arguing—and to the beginning, out of that argument, of their relationship. Dorothea wanted, then, "to make life beautiful . . . everybody's life" (153); and Will said, "The best piety is to enjoy. . . . And enjoyment radiates" (153). When I finish *Middlemarch* I feel the radiance that comes from enjoyment, and knowing from my own experience that "the effect of [Dorothea's] being on those around her [has been] incalculably diffusive," I am not depressed or saddened in the least by the reminder of "unvisited tombs" (578).

That all lives end in death is a fact no more significant than the exit off I-94 at Minneapolis. That our lives can have meaning, and that such meaning both comes from and resides in relationship is significant enough that I want both to know it and to feel it.

When Celia asks Dorothea how she can be planning to marry Will, she is asking the same question that many of George Eliot's readers ask. Dorothea's answer puzzles Celia, but it should make sense to us: "you would have to feel with me, else you would never know" (567).

· 12 ·

ENTERING PROVINCIAL LIFE

Middlemarch is a difficult novel to discuss. Just as the insensitive Jane Austen reader complains, typically, that "nothing happens" in her novels, so some readers complain that *Middlemarch* is tiresomely repetitious and dull. They hear no resonance in the repetitions of the question "What can I do?"—and they long for more liveliness and less philosophizing. For these readers Joshua Rigg's arrival in Middlemarch is a welcome surprise, and the introduction of Raffles is relief from boredom rather than intrusive plottiness. They laugh when Dorothea complains that "nobody's pig had died" (555)—as if such a trivial occurrence might make for high drama in contrast to what otherwise happens in *Middlemarch*.

George Eliot is interested in character and its development. She believes strongly that human lives are important and worthy of the closest scrutiny. Human existence is significant for us because we are ourselves human: our first concern is with our own species. Squirrels are more concerned with other squirrels than they are with birds and rabbits; a dog may ignore a passing human—but not another dog. There is something more than specific self-interest, however, in human attention to human existence, because of the kinds of choices we are able to make in our lives, and because of our necessary agreement to be responsible for those choices which we call free will. We define the responsibility of free will in moral terms, and we acknowledge the complexity of that definition in what we call character.

Character cannot be judged simply through the observation of action. Plot does not reveal character. To understand character we must keep looking at it, as closely as we can and as directly as we can. George Eliot's method as a novelist is to keep weaving and reweaving the fabric of her novel, in order to show us as richly as possible her characters' lives. She uses fine thread, but there are ever so many threads to the inch. The whole cloth is densely woven and heavily damasked. *Middlemarch* has often been called a panoramic novel, and compared with Tolstoi's *War and Peace*. But the widest panorama that George Eliot shows us is what Dorothea sees out her window on the morning after her terrible night of sorrow, in chapter 80, and *Middlemarch* is no more like *War and Peace* than Dorothea is like Saint Theresa.

The world of *Middlemarch* is relatively small, a matter of some three or four miles across except for Dorothea's honeymoon trip to Rome, and her residence with Will in London at the end of the novel. Will makes plans, once, to travel to "the Far West" (552) but does not go. Bulstrode is exiled, finally, to a coastal town (567), and Lydgate ends up splitting his time "between London and a Continental bathing place" (575). Otherwise, the world of *Middlemarch* is that of a small provincial town.

George Eliot's customary image for her way of working, of showing us the world of her novel and the people who live there, is that of a web. Sometimes she speaks more directly of how she works, without the image, telling us that we must see from changing perspectives or that she is now going to present an alternative point of view. Once, early in the novel, she explains this matter of multiple perspectives in an extended image of illumination and how it works: "Your pier-glass or extensive surface of polished steel . . . will be minutely and multitudinously scratched in all directions; but place now against it a lighted candle as a center of illumination, and lo! the scratches will seem to arrange themselves in a fine series of concentric circles round that little sun. It is demonstrable that the scratches are going everywhere impartially, and it is only your candle which produces the flattering illusion of a concentric arrangement, its light falling with an exclusive optical selection" (182). The immediate reference for this "parable" is Rosamond's "egoism"; its larger signification shows us how George Eliot fills the pages of this huge novel with the revealing details of human life. First she holds her candle in one place, and creates a focus of understanding for us; then she moves it to another place, and repeats the experiment, elucidating the same lives in another but similar situation or from another but related perspective.

Through the course of the eight books of *Middlemarch* we see Dorothea, Will, Lydgate, Rosamond, Fred, and Mary over and over again, in almost unchanging situations, doing seemingly similar or at least characteristic things. Rosamond always acts like Rosamond, never like Dorothea; Will and Lydgate and Fred are three very different people, and they act according to their different characters every time we see them. We do not get to know them any better or more profoundly through our repeated acquaintance with them, but we do become more familiar with them and can understand them both more critically and more sympathetically. Dorothea continues throughout the novel to want to "do" something, whatever the situation she is in. Will's past is discovered to him and to us, but it doesn't change him; rather, it makes sense with his character as we know it, and we thus accept that past as appropriately his. More, he responds to being told of it just as we would have expected him to.

A novelist like Dickens will rarely tell his readers much about a character when that character is introduced. Dickens is more likely to give us, in the beginning, a small tag or symbolic gesture—something representative of the character's "peculiarities and oddities"[63]—to identify him by. Then, as we become "better acquainted with him," we see this gesture elaborated into a full representation of the character and come "to know the better part of him."[64]

George Eliot does not work quite that way. She tells us more about her characters, creating them in her narrative much more than the insistently dramatic Dickens would. Dickens's characters are perhaps more exciting than George Eliot's, and certainly a great deal more goes on in his novels than in hers. But that is not to suggest that his greatest novels are any better than *Middlemarch:* they are simply different.

Middlemarch is "A Study of Provincial Life"—and that means something small and local, not grandly panoramic. *Middlemarch* is as limited, geographically and culturally and even socially, as James Joyce's *Dubliners.* And just as Joyce could call his novel a work of "moral history," so too might George Eliot call hers. Morality has to do with how we live our lives together. *Mores,* again, are those "rules of life" which we call manners or customs. What gives manners the value connotation which we intend when we speak of morality comes from the commonality of manners: not that they are ordinary or inferior, but that they are social, common to us all.

Dorothea's need to "do" something is, from the beginning, a social ambition. The more we see her anxiously pursuing that ambition the more we understand the meaning of social usefulness. Dorothea has difficulty being useful in everyday life because she does not belong to the society in which she should be living. Isolated first at Tipton Grange and then at Lowick Manor—where her husband ignores the world, where "nobody's pig had died" (555)—Dorothea cannot work for others. She has little to do. She has set up an infant school in the village, and she visits her uncle's tenants, and she draws plans for model cottages. When she can, she tries to use her money to help others—but giving people money does not in any way satisfy Dorothea's need to give herself. We keep watching her, hoping that she will find a way to participate in the world in an active social way. She has too much life and too much ambition to waste herself secluded from this world.

Lydgate never thinks in terms of morality. We realize this limitation to his ambition by comparing it to Dorothea's. Lydgate wants to "do good . . . work for Middlemarch" (102), and claims this as his professional ambition. But he is not a professional, really: his life and his work are separate things. And there is nothing social about Lydgate, either: he does what he does to please himself.

Rosamond thinks only of herself, and of the figure she makes in public. George Eliot warns us to expect little more or else from her when she describes Rosamond's education for us. At Miss Lemon's school, where "the teaching included all that was demanded in the accomplished female—even to extras, such as the getting in and out of a carriage," Rosamond is an "example," the "flower" of Miss Lemon's success (65). Rosamond's ego is sublime, thanks to Miss Lemon's efforts and her praise; Rosamond satisfies herself "in being from morning till night her own standard of a perfect lady" (115). She does not know what morality is.

Will is as concerned with himself as either Lydgate or Rosamond, when we first meet him—but his self-centeredness differs in kind from theirs because he endeavors so earnestly to be a moral man. If I argue that Will is concerned with how others see him I misrepresent the case: he is not someone who determines his values by reference to the tastes of others, but rather he maintains an almost constant critical reference to that larger world in which and to which he acknowledges his responsibility. When Will asserts his freedom—as in his assuring Dorothea that "the best piety is to enjoy" (153)—he understands freedom in a social and moral sense rather than an egotistical one.

Fred most often forgets to be moral; Mary never does. If morality were a matter of strength or physical fitness, Fred would be in training. He might even stick to it, if the training could be made simple enough. But morality requires more than simple training: it requires an ambition to be social. Fred has no such grand ambition—except for marriage to Mary. He expects to live a simple but pleasurable life in Middlemarch.

Like Fred's, Mary's ambitions extend no farther than this little

"Provincial" world. But her attitude toward the little world is different from Fred's. Mary's wisdom is that clear-eyed kind of understanding that never looks beyond her own environment, but all the same recognizes it as her environment. Mary always has enough to do; she does not need to dream of heroism.

Book 7 of *Middlemarch* is much like any of the earlier books of the novel in that it gives us yet another look at "Provincial Life." It is so heavy with the weight of Middlemarch life that there seems not even to be a scene change through its nine chapters. The Tollers have a party, and then the Vincys have a party. There is a bit of gambling—at billiards—at the Green Dragon, and a brief visit to the Garths' home. Lydgate visits Bulstrode at the bank and calls at Stone Court. Two scenes take place at Lydgate's house, followed by a scene at the Town Hall. At the very end of the book all the news from Middlemarch is taken out to Lowick, and given to Dorothea.

Middlemarch is not a very exciting place. At the party at the Tollers' there is a bit of conversation, but it is not interesting enough to stimulate even George Eliot to follow it. At the Vincys' Lydgate is "bored," and Rosamond ignores him, showing a "total absence of . . . interest in her husband's presence" (443). He leans against the mantelpiece, "showing no radiance in his face" (445). When we follow this happy couple home, they entertain us with an argument about money. As usual, Lydgate decides—egotistically—that his pleasure comes before his responsibility: he admits that their financial troubles are his fault—"I ought to have known better," he says—but then, because he "dread[s] a future without affection," he wants to pet Rosamond rather than do anything else. Rosamond, however, reflects "that the world [is] not ordered to her liking" (458) and resists.

Rosamond's egotism is outrageous: "there was but one person in Rosamond's world whom she did not regard as blameworthy, and that was the graceful creature with blond plaits and little hands crossed before her, who had never expressed herself unbecomingly, and had always acted for the best—the best naturally being what she best liked" (460). Though George Eliot inveighs with heavy-handed wit against Rosamond's self-centeredness, surely we find Lydgate's self-indulgence and irresponsible condescension even worse. His first concern is his own pleasure, just as Rosamond's is. Having grown up a Vincy, Rosamond looks to material things as the source of her pleasure. Lydgate, on the other hand, has from the beginning wanted female "adornment" for his life and has thought of his pleasure as "reclining in a paradise with sweet laughs for bird-notes, and blue eyes for a heaven" (64). Now, when he and Rosamond fight, he "carresse[s] her," and "think[s] of her as if she were an animal of another and feebler species." When we compare the two of them, we probably should find—as the lesser of two evils—that we prefer Rosamond's having "mastered" Lydgate to his "taking care" of her. When Lydgate cries, "Let us only love one another" (484) we know all too well how we must discount his appeal, and we can hardly blame Rosamond for her response.

Neither Lydgate nor Rosamond is happy or capable of being happy, because neither of them is free. Lydgate becomes "bitter" and "moody" because of the "vile yoke" of financial cares that plague him (448); "yoked" and "unhappy," he has no "free energy"—and tries both opium and gambling, pathetically, to escape (462). Rosamond is more confined: her world is more limited. She has no medical practice, no hospital or fever research, no world of ideas to which she can try to escape, nor can she go to the Green Dragon. All she can do is fight for the little world of material goods, of merchandise, by which she measures her success in life.

For the infant, the world is pre-Copernican: everything revolves around the self. Most of us grow up out of infancy, and out of infantile egotism. George Eliot calls that growth moral development. Its end is freedom, or free will. Neither Lydgate nor Rosamond ever attains this state. Trapped in self, they are both frustrated by the world external to self.

Rosamond writes to Sir Godwin, asking for money; Lydgate goes to Bulstrode. Characteristically, Lydgate resists applying to Bulstrode for aid out of pride: he has long "boasted both to himself and to others that he [is] totally independent of Bulstrode" (468). He knows that he has no other recourse than to appeal to Bulstrode, but his "repugnance" to such submission deters him (469). Finally Bulstrode himself gives Lydgate the "opportunity" to make his request. Bulstrode wants to "consult" Lydgate about his health. With that same selfishness that enabled him to turn Dorothea's earlier consultation about Casaubon's health into his request for money for his hospital, Lydgate uses "this moment in which Bulstrode [is] receiving a medical opinion . . . to make a communication of a personal need" (470). Instead of acting as a physician, Lydgate pursues his own interests. Bulstrode ignores Lydgate's request, however—the scene is that of the selfish man meeting the selfish man—and refers him back to his professional duty. Lydgate gives Bulstrode medical advice "with ill-tempered impatience"; he is angry, ironically, at "the banker's . . . intense preoccupation with himself" (471). Then, at the conclusion of their interview, Bulstrode gives Lydgate banker's advice: "My advice to you, Mr. Lydgate, would be that . . . you should simply become a bankrupt" (473).

Lydgate is already bankrupt, of course: morally bankrupt. When Bulstrode later changes his mind, lending Lydgate the money he has requested "to create in him a strong sense of personal obligation" (487), the relief from his debts does not—cannot—save Lydgate. He has never been truly free, because he has never understood freedom. Now he belongs both to Bulstrode and to Rosamond. He is a slave— and a slave, by definition, cannot be a professional man.

When Lydgate attends the sanitary meeting at the Town Hall, he does so in his professional capacity. Middlemarch is worried about "the occurrence of a cholera case in the town" (501). But instead of talking about medical sanitation, the meeting turns to moral sanitation, and Bulstrode is exposed. Lydgate is as furious as anyone at what he hears, but the "instinct of the Healer" checks his hatred (502). It is only "instinct," however, which checks his anger: when Bulstrode rises feebly to leave the meeting, Lydgate does not *want* to help him. He feels "unspeakably bitter" that his professional obligation requires him to do what "instinct" tells him what he must do: "He could not see a man sink close to him for want of help. He rose and gave his arm to Bulstrode" (504).

Lydgate acts, not out of sympathy or even out of duty. His concern for Bulstrode's situation is overshadowed by his sense of his own plight. Were he able to act according to either thought or desire, Lydgate would not help Bulstrode at all. His assistance to the stricken banker to whom he is in debt is neither moral nor free: it is purely instinctual.

At the end of Book 7 Brooke and Farebrother bring the news of the meeting at the Town Hall to Dorothea at Lowick. Her response— the manner of her response to someone else's trouble—is completely different from Lydgate's. It is typical of Dorothea, true to her character. At the same time it is going to cause a change in Dorothea, by taking her actively into the world. When Brooke and Featherstone tell her the story, Dorothea "listen[s] with deep interest, and beg[s] to hear twice over the facts and impressions concerning Lydgate." She listens sympathetically—and though one might sometimes argue that sympathy is Dorothea's natural instinct, her keen interest in this story is not merely instinct. When she has thought about what she has been told, she turns to Farebrother and says, "You don't believe that Mr. Lydgate is guilty of anything base? I will not believe it. Let us find out the truth and clear him" (505). To Dorothea, clearing Lydgate of suspicion is a matter of duty, and she is characteristically eager to assume the responsibility she sees as offered to her. It is also characteristic of Dorothea to assume that Lydgate is innocent, and that "the truth" will in fact "clear him."

What Dorothea undertakes, however, is not the discovery of "the truth" about Lydgate. She is not a detective, but a sympathetic believer. To understand better what she proposes to do we might recall certain phrases from the Prelude. There George Eliot warned us of what to expect for her heroine: "no epic life," "spiritual grandeur ill-matched with the meanness of opportunity" (xiii). Dorothea's "ardently willing soul" sees in Lydgate's situation the chance to "do" something; and though what she will do is but a "vague ideal" (xiii), she is ready to set out into the world on his behalf.

Whatever "the truth" about Lydgate is, Dorothea does not succeed in saving him. But that is not important, finally. No one could save Lydgate. He causes his own failure and defeats himself. Even he realizes how unworthy he is of Dorothea's noble and courageous faith in him.

Middlemarch is not a novel about what Dorothea accomplishes in the world, though it is important that she go into it. The story that began as "Miss Brooke" is still about Miss Brooke even as it becomes "A Novel called Middlemarch."[65] The great accomplishment of the novel is Dorothea herself, not what she does: it is her life in this world that matters: her existence among us. Her success begins, in a sense, with her determination to enter the world on Lydgate's behalf.

· 13 ·

RADIANCE

In the end, *Middlemarch* is a powerful, movingly beautiful, and radical love story. Book 8 begins with Dorothea's finding, at last, something worthy to do, and determining to do it whether anyone agrees with her or not. Her "impetuous generosity" of spirit refuses the checks of more conservative advisors. She rejects their "cautious weighing of consequences." Dorothea "feel[s] convinced" of Lydgate's innocence, and makes up her mind to prove that innocence to others; thus her great question—"What do we live for, if it is not to make life less difficult to each other?" (506)—constitutes an assertion of heroic free will.

Dorothea began the novel assuming that the reason for our human existence was "to make life less difficult to each other," but she couldn't find anything important to do toward that end. She has not changed: when she articulates this principle to Farebrother, her "tone and manner [are] not more energetic than they had been when she was at the head of her uncle's table nearly three years before." But Dorothea's "experience since [has] given her more right to express a decided opinion," and she is suddenly on her own, acting independently (506–

07). Sir James believes that if Lydgate can "clear himself, he . . . must act for himself"; Farebrother counsels caution, and warns Dorothea that Lydgate may not be as guiltless as she presumes him to be. Dorothea answers that she is not "afraid of asking Mr. Lydgate to tell [her] the truth." She wants to help Lydgate, and is unwilling to accept pusillanimous advice. She is ready for that grandest of heroic actions, called kindness or fellow-feeling, active sympathy or simple love of neighbor: "People glorify all sorts of bravery except the bravery they might show on behalf of their nearest neighbours" (507).

Dorothea almost converts Farebrother with her "ardour," and he remarks that "a woman may venture on some effects of sympathy which would hardly succeed if we men undertook them." Sir James is unmoved, however: "a woman," he says, "is bound to be cautious and listen to those who know the world better than she does" (507). Celia, the professional wife, agrees; she considers it "a mercy" that Dorothea has Sir James "to think for" her (508).

Farebrother's remark is sexist in that it assumes that sympathy belongs to women, and not to men, in an effective sense. In George Eliot's eyes, such a view is unfair to men. Farebrother also thinks that there are things that men can do which are larger and greater than what can be accomplished through female sympathy. To George Eliot, that is unfair not just to women but to human existence. When they were in Rome earlier, Will criticized Dorothea for what he called "the fanaticism of sympathy" (152). Her sympathy interfered with her enjoyment of life, Will said; and according to his philosophy, "The best piety is to enjoy. You are doing the most then to save the earth's character as an agreeable planet. And enjoyment radiates" (153). Will is right at that point—about sympathy, and maybe about Dorothea's "fanaticism." But now her sympathy is at one with her enjoyment, and those who would limit her in exercising it would restrict her effective life.

Dorothea does help Lydgate with her sympathy, and then she helps Rosamond. At the end of the novel, it is her sympathy that lets her love and marry Will, and it radiates "incalculably" in the world around her. Her "work" then is—as Caleb Garth's is—her "delight" (571).

Sir James's simple sexism does not even consider the worth of sympathy. He presumes that men, because they are men, "know the world better" than women do. And poor, thoughtless Celia agrees; she likes the idea of a husband to do her thinking for her. Frustrated, Dorothea exclaims, "As if I wanted a husband! . . . I only want not to have my feelings checked at every turn" (508).

Dorothea does not want—in either sense of the word, desire or lack—a husband. In both senses, however, she does want love. But that is something quite different; it is neither sexist nor demeaning to want love. *Middlemarch* is not a novel about marriage any more than Jane Austen's novels are. There is nothing wrong, however, with the idea of marriage. "What do we live for, if it is not to make life less difficult to each other?" is a question about the ideal of human relationship. Marriage is—or can be, or should be—such a relationship. In our culture, despite the disvaluing concept of the "significant other," marriage is still the standard symbol of relationship. By looking at marriage, we can perhaps see how all kinds of relationships do or do not work. By focusing our attention more precisely on the idea of relationship itself—on what the parties involved want or expect—we can see what they value in life.

Lydgate is frustrated: "He had meant everything to turn out differently," including the marriage which he now sees as "unmitigated calamity." But he never blames himself for his troubles: "others had thrust themselves into his life, and thwarted his purpose" (509). Blaming the world for his dissatisfaction, Lydgate acts exactly like Rosamond. She complained, earlier, of "disagreeable people who only thought of themselves, and did not mind how annoying they were to her" (460), and objected that "the world was not ordered to her liking" (448). That neither Lydgate nor Rosamond can share anything demonstrates how petty and selfish their ways of seeing life are. They cannot even share their mutual grief. "How would Rosamond take it all?" Lydgate asks himself; "He had no impulse to tell her the trouble

Radiance

which must soon be common to them both. He preferred waiting for the incidental disclosure which events must soon bring about" (511).

Rosamond finds out from her father and is shocked: "It seemed to her that no lot could be so cruelly hard as hers." She is outraged not because she has married a man who has done wrong, but because she has "married a man who [has] become the centre of infamous suspicion" (522) and thus embarrasses her.

Rosamond tells herself that it is Lydgate's obligation to speak first: "Whatever was to be said . . . she expected to come from Tertius." She interprets his "reserve and want of confidence" as evidence against him: "if he were innocent of any wrong, why did he not do something to clear himself?" (522–23). Lydgate, for his part, waits in "the bitterness of his soul" for Rosamond to speak. Repressing his "deeper-lying consciousness that he was at fault" for not confiding in her, he complains: "If she has any trust in me . . . she ought to speak now and say that she does not believe that I have deserved disgrace." Refusing to communicate with each other, refusing the relationship in which they are bound, Rosamond and Lydgate exist "as if they were both adrift on one piece of wreck and looked away from each other" (522–23).

Conversation is not easy. Even the most humane and understanding of us fail sometimes to say what we need to say, what needs to be said. At our best, however, we overcome our pride or pain or fear and speak. Because Bulstrode is ashamed and afraid to speak to his wife, Harriet has to learn of what has happened from Middlemarch: "a wife could not long remain ignorant that the town held a bad opinion of her husband" (511). First Mrs. Hackbutt, then Mrs. Plymdale, and finally her brother tell her what has happened and what Bulstrode is accused of in the public eye. She goes home, weak and sick at heart. She retires to her room; she needs "time to get used to her maimed consciousness" of her life with Bulstrode. However "imperfectly-taught" (517) Mrs. Bulstrode is, she knows not to "forsake" her husband now that he needs her: "She knew, when she locked her door, that she would unlock it ready to go down to her unhappy husband

and espouse his sorrow. . . . But she needed time to gather up her strength" (518).

Like Lydgate, Bulstrode has been unable to communicate his disaster to his wife; and "now that he imagine[s] the moment of her knowledge come, he await[s] the result in anguish." But she does not accuse or berate him: "A movement of new compassion and old kindness [goes] through her like a great wave." She asks him to "look up" at her; otherwise they don't speak. She touches him "gently," and "they [cry] together, she sitting by his side." "His confession [is] silent, and her promise of faithfulness [is] silent" (518); and they achieve a communion that will enable them to continue their lives together. Because of Harriet Bulstrode's love and sympathy and human decency, perhaps Bulstrode will become a better man. He certainly cannot be a worse man for having such a wife.

Lydgate finally forms in his mind the "intention of opening" himself to Rosamond, but he is too late. Rosamond, too, has been considering, and she speaks first. Her understanding is not a communication; it is a demand, a statement of doctrinal selfishness: "I cannot go on living here. . . . Whatever misery I have to put up with, it will be easier away from here" (523).

Despite Sir James's and Farebrother's warnings—and Brooke's, that "It is easy to go too far, you know" (508)—Dorothea "summons" Lydgate and begins her work in the world. She explains herself and her interest in her usual way at first: "I have very little to do." She wants to "clear" his name and tells him, "There is nothing better that I can do in the world." Dorothea so moves Lydgate with this proposal that "for the first time in his life" he accepts "generous sympathy, without any check of proud reserve" (526).

Dorothea tries to help Lydgate with her sympathetic understanding, but he cannot be helped. "I had some ambition," he says; "I meant everything to be different with me" (527). Dorothea offers both her goodness and her money (528) and urges Lydgate to "do what [he] meant to do." Echoing her earlier plea to Casaubon, she encourages Lydgate to do what is necessary to make "his knowledge useful." He has it "in [his] power to do great things." But Lydgate cannot do anything. He excuses himself, saying "It is impossible for me to do anything without considering my wife's happiness" (528). He opts for the "easier" course, which is to "do as other men do, and think what will please the world and bring in money" (530).

Dorothea responds boldly to this pathetic performance. She has a new "plan" (530): she will give Lydgate the money he has borrowed from Bulstrode, and she will visit Rosamond. Her idea is at once to free Lydgate from his debt and to demonstrate to Rosamond her faith in him. Her "plan," however, doesn't work. There is an interference. Though Dorothea "has less outward vision than usual" (534) when she goes to see Rosamond, she does see Will in Rosamond's drawing-room, holding Rosamond's hands and speaking "with low-toned fervour" (534).

Dorothea leaves the letter for Lydgate, and her check. She goes then to Freshitt Hall, "to carry out the purpose with which she had started in the morning," which is to try to persuade Sir James and Brooke of Lydgate's innocence (535). But there is still a serious interference. She arrives even "more ardent in readiness to be [Lydgate's] champion" than she was before—but she doesn't know why this is so, or what she might say on his behalf.

Celia exclaims, "Dodo, how very bright your eyes are! . . . And you don't see a thing you look at." Celia senses that "something [has] happened," and that her sister is about "to do something uncomfortable." Dorothea agrees that "a great many things have happened"— but then, to explain, she refers grandly to "all the troubles of all the people on the face of the earth" (535). What Dorothea means in saying this is of the utmost importance to the novel. Dorothea has finally admitted to her own feelings, though she cannot quite call them her own yet. She expresses her pain at seeing Will and Rosamond together as "all the troubles of all the people on the face of the earth." Ordinarily, we would criticize such exaggeration and transference as egotistical; for Dorothea, however, it is literally wonderful, and signifies her full membership in this world.

Dorothea cannot yet admit to herself that she loves Will. After all, that is forbidden to her by Casaubon's will. Her impulse always is to efface self and consider the world. But this time she has not seen the world suffering; she has seen what may add to Lydgate's troubles, if Rosamond is really involved with Will, but that is not the main thing she has discovered in seeing Will and Rosamond together. She has seen her own hurt, her own trouble—and she generalizes that into "all the troubles of all the people on the face of the earth" (535). When she is alone, later that evening, she moans to herself, "Oh, I did love him" (542).

This admission brings on "waves of suffering" that shake Dorothea "too thoroughly to leave any power of thought" (542). She sobs herself to sleep on the floor of her room. She awakens the next morning "to a new condition: she [feels] as if her soul [has] been liberated from its terrible conflict," and she can now make her "grief . . . a sharer of her thoughts." Having submitted to her feelings—of love and what she thinks is betrayal—she awakens cleansed. She has not harbored her hurt or her anger at Will; she has not indulged in feelings of self-justification. Now "the thoughts c[o]me quickly," and she returns in her mind to that scene which caused her pain: "She [begins] now to live through that yesterday morning deliberately again, forcing herself to dwell on every detail and its possible meaning." Thoughtfully, Dorothea sees through her own hurt to Rosamond's situation. The scene which caused Dorothea grief is "bound up in another woman's life" (543). Determining to "clutch [her] own pain, and compel it to silence," she resolves to "do" something to be "helpful" (544).

George Eliot rewards Dorothea's heroic resolution by giving her the vision she has so long wanted: "She opened her curtains, and looked out toward the bit of road that lay in view, with fields beyond, outside the entrance-gates. On the road there was a man with a bundle on his back and a woman carrying her baby; in the field she could see figures moving—perhaps the shepherd with his dog. Far off in the bending sky was the pearly light; and she felt the largeness of the world and the manifold wakings of men to labour and endurance"

(544). Dorothea looks out on this symbolic world and understands its largeness. Moreover, she knows herself to be "a part of that involuntary, palpitating life," and accepts it (544).

Earlier, Dorothea has thought to use her money to make a little world of her own, "a little colony, where everybody should work, and all the work should be done well" (380). The scheme sounds not just Utopian, but outrageously Faustian—even to her plan "to drain" the land. She expects to "know every one of the people and be their friend" (380)—and to play queen of the pet-shop, or proprietress of an English Eden. Much better—and much grander—that Dorothea should become involved in the large world. And much better for George Eliot, too, to reward her heroine for wanting to be "helpful" to those around her by letting her see the "largeness of the world," and herself "a part of [its] life" (544).

But for all that this vision shows Dorothea, "What she would resolve to do that day [does] not yet seem quite clear" (544). When she sets out late that morning to make "her second attempt to see and save Rosamond," all she knows is that she will speak to her. Dorothea concludes the first portion of her address, concerning Lydgate and her belief in his innocence, with a characteristic question: "How can we live and think that anyone has trouble—piercing trouble—and we can help them, and never try?" (548). The second part is more difficult; Dorothea feels "a great wave of her own sorrow returning over her" as she begins to speak about Rosamond herself, and Will.

If we read only plot, we could argue that Dorothea's attempt to "save Rosamond" is a selfish act: that she wants to save Rosamond's marriage to Lydgate in order to reclaim Will for herself. George Eliot does not allow us to misread Dorothea's generosity in this way, however; the scene insists in its every detail on Dorothea's goodness. As she tries to warn Rosamond "the waves of her own sorrow . . . rush over her"—but "out of [that sorrow] she [is] struggling to save" Rosamond. And as Dorothea speaks, her emotion so communicates itself to Rosamond that she is transformed by it: Rosamond is "taken hold of by an emotion stronger than her own," and she "deliver[s] her soul under impulses which she [has] not known before" (550). Dorothea's generosity changes Rosamond, momentarily. But Rosamond's goodness is only "a reflex of [Dorothea's] own energy" (551), and it does not last. Rosamond knows—feels—how good and beautiful Dorothea is and seems to accept Lydgate again. In the finale, however, we are told the rest of their story, and find that Lydgate and Rosamond have in the end failed both Dorothea's great effort and themselves.

Though her heroics do not affect Lydgate and Rosamond in any lasting way, they do affect Dorothea herself: she has "a great deal of superfluous strength" in the aftermath of her visit to Rosamond. But though she has "more strength than she [can] manage," nothing needs "to be done in the village": "Everybody was well and had flannel; nobody's pig had died" (555).

There are still problems in the large world, however, and there is still the problem of Dorothea's loving Will to be solved. Dorothea tries to avoid it by "self-discipline," and determines "to study" something. With awful irony she chooses the geography of Asia Minor (555)—which takes her all the way back to Casaubon. But then Will comes to visit her, and a different kind of self-discipline becomes necessary. By the end of the scene, Dorothea has claimed him with her love.

At the beginning of the novel Dorothea gave up jewels because she did not want them—in either sense of the word. She possessed them, but she did not desire them. Now she gives up wealth. She does not want wealth either: she has it, but she does not desire it. She wants happiness, and love. Happiness and love can give a purpose to life; wealth can't. And because Dorothea wants a purpose in life—is determined, from first to last, to find something "to do"—she performs what to our society is the terribly radical act of giving up her wealth. She exchanges her wealth for love. Oddly, such an exchange is so simple and wise that we probably do not want to call it heroic.

But the world does not grow better or wiser easily, and "the Lords [throw] out the Reform Bill" (561). After all, we do not want to "go too far," or "let [our] ideas run away" with us (508). Wealthy young women of good family going about giving up fortunes to marry sons of pawnbrokers are disturbing political economy—and threatening the survival of the nation.

Yet some things do change, and in the next year—the year in which Dorothea and Will marry—the Reform Bill is passed, and English society takes what some would regard as a huge step forward. For George Eliot, however, political reform is not all that important: "reforms . . . were begun" in Will's and Dorothea's time "with a young hopefulness of immediate good"; but that good "has been much checked in our days." Dorothea is pleased when Will is finally returned to Parliament, that "since wrongs existed . . . her husband should be in the thick of the struggle against them" (576); George Eliot, however, is more pleased that Dorothea herself is engaged in this world's struggle not only against wrongs but for that greatest right that she calls at once "duty" and "sympathy."

It does not matter that the "fine tissues" of Dorothea's goodness are "not widely visible," because "the growing good of the world is partly dependent on unhistoric acts." Dorothea does not need to "do" anything, finally: "the effect of her being on those around her [is] incalculably diffusive" (578). Will understands this influence when he tells Dorothea, early in the novel, that she is a "poem" (156): he loves works of art, and like George Eliot he believes that art can "enlarge men's sympathies." "When you feel delight," Will says, "in art or anything else," that "enjoyment radiates" (153).

Middlemarch has been moving toward this end ever since "Miss Brooke" was introduced to us. At the beginning we were warned not to expect too much success for Dorothea. The Prelude ends with a description of that modern "Saint Theresa, foundress of nothing, whose loving heart-beats and sobs after an unattained goodness tremble off and are dispersed among hinderances" (xiv). The epigraph for the opening chapter is a limiting quotation taken—significantly—from Beaumont and Fletcher's *The Maid's Tragedy*. By the time we reach the Finale, however, we believe against the narrator's testing of our faith: the limitations which she acknowledges for Dorothea are not as serious as they seem, given the freedom that Dorothea has achieved and the goodness which radiates from it. The "determining acts of her life"—most notably her marriage to Casaubon—have not been "ideally beautiful"; she has made mistakes, the "result of young and noble impulse struggling amidst the conditions of an imperfect social state"; and she has been limited to some extent—as we all are—by the world she lives in (578). No "new Theresa," George Eliot says, "will have the opportunity of reforming a conventual life," nor will a "new Antigone" find occasion for such heroism as the past offered her. But none of this matters. Dorothea is heroic—and we affirm her heroism with George Eliot when she concludes that "the effect of [Dorothea's] being on those around her was incalculably diffusive" (578).

Even without that wonderful final sentence of this long novel, I would still resist any negative assessment of Dorothea's significance in this world because of what her life means to us. What she does or should do in Middlemarch or in London is no more important that what she does in our world, for us. Dorothea *is* a poem: Will is right. And art's great achievement is "to enlarge men's sympathies."

But why does Dorothea so affect us? The answer is a simple one. The ardent young woman who spends most of the novel wanting "to do" something heroic or grand hit first on the idea of an "infant school," and then on a "plan" for model cottages; she had ideas, too, about marriage—that "the really delightful marriage must be that where your husband was a sort of father, and could teach you Hebrew, if you wished it" (4). By the end of the novel she has married a young man—the son of a Jewish pawnbroker, but not a teacher of Hebrew, and her lover instead of her father. She establishes a home of her own and raises her own infants. Dorothea loves her Will freely, and he loves her: "They [are] bound to each other by a love stronger than any impulse which could have marred it" (576).

Like all great stories, the end of *Middlemarch* is its own. But since we have talked about free will before, and used *The Divine Comedy* to elucidate the argument, let me use Dante once more now, to explain what I mean about the serene triumph of love with which *Middlemarch* ends. At the conclusion of *The Divine Comedy*, at the very top of Paradise, Dante expects to see God. This ideal vision is to be his reward for the struggle up from the dark wood in which he began. As he yearns toward this supreme understanding, suddenly he sees through the idea of God, and comprehends not God Himself but the universe: he feels himself a part of that universe, moved freely—desire and intellect acting together now—"by the Love that moves the sun and the other stars."[66]

Dorothea's grand ambition, like Dante's, fulfills itself in simple things, like love. Her triumph is in this world, and in her being a part of this world. She is not a queen, finally, or the Virgin Mary, or Antigone, or Saint Theresa. She is Dorothea, a lovely, loving woman whose goodness should inspire us.

The finale tells us first of Fred and Mary, then of Lydgate and Rosamond, and then of Will and Dorothea. Fred's and Mary's story is an easy one, soothingly comic at the end just as we have always known it must be. The ironic reversal that Middlemarch contrives to understand the authorship of their books is part of the happy comedy, which concludes with our seeing "the two lovers" at Stone Court "on sunny days . . . in white-haired placidity at the open window" (575).

Lydgate's and Rosamond's story also ends as we have long known it must, but its ending is painful and nasty. Lydgate dies a failure, and Rosamond lives on in haughty, wealthy self-congratulation.

Will's and Dorothea's story ends beautifully. When George Eliot describes the love that binds them to each other, she celebrates their growth and change. Will has found something "to do," and has taken up Dorothea's commitment "to make life beautiful" (152), by working as an "ardent public man" (576). Dorothea has learned to "enjoy" life, by learning to love; and the life that she lives, then, "radiates" her goodness (153) so that its effect is "incalculably diffusive" (578).

Middlemarch began with "Miss Brooke" on the verge of "going into society" (7). For much of the novel Dorothea is cut off from society, however, isolated from the world that she needs to know and in which she wants to work. Eventually she finds her way "into society" in a real and significant sense, first by helping Lydgate and Rosamond, and then by loving Will. Love, after all, is a profoundly social act.

In the end there remain people in Middlemarch who cannot understand Dorothea, and many people in the world of the novel who do not even know her, who have never heard of her. But those of us who, in our own world, know her must surely love her—and our own lives must be changed and enlarged by that relationship. If we cannot figure out exactly why this is so, we might recall that—as Will said— Dorothea is a poem. And understanding a work of art requires both thought and feeling. As Dorothea tells Celia, concerning her love for Will, "you would have to feel . . . else you would never know" (517).

Student Responses to *Middlemarch*

The following brief comments were written by students in my *Middlemarch* class at The University of Michigan in the fall of 1986. The course was a lecture course; so that the students could contribute to the class, they wrote "scribbles" for five minutes at the end of each hour. I collected these, read them, scribbled back in response, and returned them at the start of the next hour. I have chosen a small sample of what seemed to me the best ones: the most thoughtful and productive ones, the ones that perhaps George Eliot would have been proud to have provoked in students of her work.

•   •   •

Though Casaubon is wrapped up in his own needs and desires, he has a chance at life because his spouse has so much to offer him. But Casaubon rejects Dorothea's spirit and goodness, and becomes more and more entrenched in his old ways. The reader keeps hoping that Casaubon will be able to learn something from his wife, but he doesn't. And he is at fault for his own failure. The situation of Lydgate and Rosamond is much worse. They are forever hopeless. They have no mentors or examples to guide them. They have only each other—and the reader, therefore, has no hope or expectation for them.

Felice Sheramy

•   •   •

Lydgate seems to be a noble creature because he so wants to cure his patients, relieve their pain. He takes pride in his ambition, and becomes self-satisfied. But Lydgate helps people to help himself. His intent in life is not "to make life less difficult" to others; making life less difficult is merely a means to an end for Lydgate. Dorothea, however, helps people because she sympathizes with their pain.

Jeana Lee

. . .

In Book IV, Will tells Dorothea about his mother's being disinherited for her "*mésalliance.*" Dorothea's response is to wonder "how she bore the change from wealth to poverty . . . was she happy with her husband." She is thinking, of course, of her own unhappy marriage. She knows that money doesn't make one happy, but she isn't sure whether the lack of money makes one unhappy. Rosamond, on the other hand, upon hearing from Lydgate of Dorothea's devotion to Casaubon, thinks "it was not so very melancholy to be mistress of Lowick Manor with a husband likely to die soon." Rosamond is sure that money is the only factor in Dorothea's presumed happiness. In the end, Dorothea will take the chance on "poverty," in marrying Will; Rosamond always bets on money.

Bill Telgen

. . .

Lydgate's materialism is not his character flaw; it's just a symptom of what's wrong with him. He fails because of his over-confidence, his lack of will-power, and his lack of real principles. And even though he ends up a fairly wealthy man—rich enough to satisfy Rosamond, anyway—he still considers himself a failure because he didn't achieve what he set out to achieve. His professional ambitions were not materialistic—and they were not sidetracked by materialistic desires. It wasn't greed that distracted and defeated Lydgate, nor was it his marriage to a materialistic wife. For all that Lydgate considered himself a man of purpose, it was his pathetic lack of serious purpose that ruined him. It is this weakness in Lydgate that lets us sympathize with him rather than condemn him. He blames and condemns himself for wasting his life.

Brendan Mahaney

•   •   •

Dorothea's emphasis on feeling over knowledge suggests the importance of viewing knowledge as a tool rather than an end in itself. Casaubon's work on the "Key to All Mythologies" is an example of the accumulation of knowledge: inert, sterile, useless. But the "knowledge passing into feeling" which Dorothea experiences transforms the raw materials of knowledge into useful tools—wisdom, compassion, love—with which we can enrich our world.

Ted Moncreiff

•   •   •

"To ask her to be less simple and direct would be like breathing on the crystal that you wanted to see the light through." This is an unvoiced thought of Will's regarding Dorothea. Dorothea thinks in very simple terms. Even when she has matured, grown out of that naive innocence or blindness that let her marry Casaubon, she still thinks with the frank, open mind of a child. Her ideal thoughts about human existence come from this open-mindedness toward everything she encounters. If more of us could manage such open-mindedness, we might come up with new ideas and new ways of doing things which could make this world a little better.

Andy Walker

•   •   •

In Dorothea's opinion people may have vocations in them that are not yet apparent, to themselves or to others. Will Ladislaw is alive to every opportunity he encounters in politics and the arts. But his dabbling should not be viewed as dilettanteish; rather, his dabbles should be seen as abortive attempts to find that vocation which will use both his intellectual and his imaginative or emotional capabilities. Lydgate—who is satisfied with himself and his profession—is much more the dilettante. He dabbles with marriage—and ends up forsaking the great vocation he was so sure of.

Rosanne Walker

• • •

Will is the antithesis of both Lydgate and Casaubon. Lydgate is the head of the hospital, and plans to do "great work for the world." Casaubon has his "Key to All Mythologies" as his life's work, and is utterly absorbed in it. Will, however, is unemployed, and unsettled; he has as yet no definite goal in life.

We see the contrast between Will and the other two again in their treatment of Dorothea. Her husband sees her as a bother. Lydgate sees her as a simpleton who tries to do good but will never succeed. Will sees her as a "poem"—which takes in knowledge and turns it into feeling, a form of love.

Mark Shaiman

• • •

Lydgate has a tremendous amount of knowledge, but no wisdom. Ditto Casaubon. Even though Dorothea is always apologizing for not knowing Latin or Greek, she has a great deal more wisdom than either of them. And throughout the novel she changes, grows, and becomes more wise. Brooke knows a lot about art, and finds it pleasing—but Dorothea doesn't. Dorothea expects art to convey meaning, and express human sympathy, and make us wise. George Eliot agrees with

Dorothea, and though she is very knowledgable about a number of things, what is valuable is her wisdom. She is really quite inspiring. She gives the reader a good feeling about life, a hope that even though things will never be perfect we can strive for better lives and for a better world.

Jennifer Johnson

• • •

"It is one thing to like defiance and another to like its consequences." Dorothea is defiant, and acts—or tries to act—to reform things by starting a school, building low-income housing, etc. She undertakes such acts, intending their consequences to be positive. Will is defiant, as illustrated by his political writings; but he doesn't care, really, about the consequences. Lydgate is defiant of the rest of the local medical community. His defiance is haughty, selfish, and self-righteous; he doesn't think of the consequences.

Isn't wanting to "enlarge men's sympathies" a sort of defiance? What are the consequences of such? I think George Eliot wants us to change the world, to make it easier and better and more beautiful for all of us.

Michael Corbett

• • •

Middlemarch is anywhere. It's Ann Arbor, my home in Cincinnati, the world. When you hear someone saying "We're here to make life easier for each other," it strikes at your heart. But so many of us don't—or won't live that way. And it rubs off—makes you greedy, like all the people at old Featherstone's funeral.

My favorite contemporary artist is Pete Townsend. One of his songs says, "It's sympathy, not tears, people need when they're the front page of sad news." I never understood what he meant. I thought sympathy and tears were the same thing. But I know better now—

after Dorothea and *Middlemarch*. Sympathy is not a sign of sorrow, but of greater understanding.

Dorothea is a wonderful woman. So is Mary. I like Will, too— and Mr. Garth. It's great when he says he forgives Fred. "You have to forgive young people when they are sorry." That's beautiful. You wouldn't expect to hear Casaubon say such a thing.

To say that this novel is moving is a great compliment to it. I guess I ought not be afraid to say that.

Robert Gavin

Notes

1. R. Keith, in his translation of E. W. Hengstenberg's *Christology of the Old Testament* (1836), 1:114. Quoted in the *Oxford English Dictionary* (Compact edition), 1:606.

2. Letter to Robert Evans, 28 February 1842. *The George Eliot Letters*, ed. Gordon S. Haight (New Haven: Yale University Press, 1954–55), 1:128.

3. T. B. Macaulay, "Southey's *Colloquies on Society*," *Edinburgh Review* 100 (January 1830), 565. Rprt. in *Complete Works of T. B. Macaulay* (Philadelphia: University Library Association, 1910), 13:143.

4. Elizabeth Longford, *Queen Victoria: Born to Succeed* (New York: Harper and Row, 1964), 224.

5. Letter to Charles Bray, 5 July 1859, *Letters* 3:111.

6. Virginia Woolf, *Times Literary Supplement*, 20 November 1919, 657.

7. Ibid.

8. *Saturday Review* 23 (7 December 1872), 733.

9. *Fortnightly Review* 19 (19 January 1873), 142–44.

10. *Galaxy* 15 (March 1873), 424–27.

11. *Academy* 1 (1 January 1875), 2–4.

12. Joseph Jacobs, *Essays and Reviews* (London: Macmillan, 1891), 39–41.

13. Leslie Stephen, *George Eliot* (London: Macmillan, 1902), 183–84.

14. Woolf, *Times Literary Supplement*, 658.

15. David Cecil, *Early Victorian Novelists* (New York: Bobbs Merrill, 1935), 317, 328, 335.

16. F. R. Leavis, *The Great Tradition* (London: Chatto and Windus, 1948), 61, 79.

17. Lee R. Edwards, "Women, Energy, and Middlemarch," *Massachusetts Review* 13 (1972), 235–36.

18. Woolf, *Times Literary Supplement* 657.

19. Elaine Showalter, *A Literature of Their Own* (Princeton: Princeton University Press, 1977), 107–08.

20. Ibid., 111–12.

21. J. Hillis Miller, "Optic and Semiotic in *Middlemarch*," *The Worlds of Victorian Fiction*, ed. Jerome H. Buckley (Cambridge: Harvard University Press, 1975), 126–30, 143–44. See also Miller's "Narrative and History," *ELH* 41 (Fall 1974), 455–73.

22. Kerry McSweeney, *Middlemarch* (London: Allen and Unwin, 1984), 150.

23. Journal, 31 December 1870, *Letters* 5:127.

24. Letter to John Blackwood, 7 May 1871, *Letters* 5:146.

25. Letter to Charles Bray, 5 July 1859, *Letters* 3:111.

26. "Silly Novels by Lady Novelists," *Westminster Review* 66 (October 1856), 461.

27. "Quarry for *Middlemarch*" was first published in *Nineteenth Century Fiction*, suppl. to vol. 4 (1950), ed. Anna T. Kitchel; rprt. in the Norton Critical Edition of *Middlemarch* (New York: W. W. Norton, 1977).

28. Thomas Hardy, *Tess of the D'Urbervilles* (Baltimore: Penguin Books, 1978), 180.

29. Walter Pater, *The Renaissance* (New York: Meridian Books, 1961), 222.

30. Ibid., 113.

31. Letter to Frederic Harrison, 15 August 1866, *Letters* 4:300.

32. P. B. Shelley, "A Defense of Poetry" (1840), paragraph 3.

33. Letter to Mme. Eugène Bodichon, 26 December 1860, *Letters* 3:366.

34. Jacobs, *Essays and Reviews*, 72.

35. Letter to Dante Gabriel Rossetti, 8 May 1870, *Letters* 5:93.

36. *Essays and Leaves from a Notebook*, ed. Charles Lee Lewes (London: Blackwood, 1884), 353.

37. Matthew Arnold, "On Poetry," *The Complete Prose Works of Matthew Arnold*, ed. R. H. Super (Ann Arbor: University of Michigan Press, 1973), 9:62.

38. Pater, *The Renaissance*, 126.

39. John Keats, *Selected Poems and Letters*, ed. Douglas Bush (Cambridge: Houghton-Mifflin, 1959), 138.

40. Quoted in Thomas Pinney, "More Leaves from George Eliot's Notebook," *Huntington Library Quarterly* 22 (1966), 364.

41. Letter to Frederic Harrison, 15 August 1866, *Letters* 4:300.

Notes

42. F. W. H. Myers, *Essays—Modern* (London: Macmillan, 1883), 268–69.

43. Ibid.

44. Letter to Clifford Allbutt, August 1868, *Letters* 4:472.

45. Ibid.

46. Aeschylus, *Agamemnon*, 1. 177.

47. Letter to Sara Sophia Hennell, 9 October 1843, *Letters* 1:162.

48. Thomas Carlyle, "Shooting Niagara: And After?" *Collected Works*, vol. 9 (London: Chapman and Hill, 1869), 340–41. Rprt. with additions from *Macmillan's Magazine* 16 (August 1867).

49. *Felix Holt the Radical* (Baltimore: Penguin Books, 1966), 368.

50. Ibid., 367.

51. John Ruskin, *Munera Pulveris, Fraser's Magazine* 65 (1862), 47. Rprt. in *Ruskin's Works* (Boston: Dana Estes, 19—), 15:111.

52. Ibid.

53. Ruskin, *Unto This Last, Cornhill Magazine* 2 (1860), 559. Rprt. in *Ruskin's Works*, 6:219.

54. Letter to Charles Bray, 5 July 1859, *Letters* 3:111.

55. George Henry Lewes to John Blackwood, 7 September 1871, *Letters* 5:184.

56. George Henry Lewes to William Blackwood, 11 September 1871, *Letters* 5:185.

57. L. M. Langford to John Blackwood, 15 September 1871, *Letters* 5:188.

58. Letter to Francois d'Albert-Durade, 29 January 1872, *Letters* 5:241.

59. P. B. Shelley, "A Defense of Poetry," paragraph 39.

60. Charles Dickens, *David Copperfield* (Baltimore: Penguin Books, 1966), 49.

61. Dante Alighieri, *Purgatorio*, canto 18.

62. "The Natural History of German Life," *Westminster Review* 66 (July 1856), 28.

63. Dickens, *Pickwick Papers* (Baltimore: Penguin Books, 1972), 45.

64. Ibid.

65. Journal, 1 January 1869, *Letters* 5:3.

66. Dante Alighieri, *Paradiso*, canto 33.

Bibliography

Primary Sources

Middlemarch was first published in eight parts, between December 1871 and December 1872. It was reissued in four volumes in 1872 and again in 1873. In 1874 it was reprinted, with corrections by the author.

George Eliot gave the title *Quarry for "Middlemarch"* to the small notebook which she used in planning the novel. This notebook was first published in 1950, in an edition prepared by Professor Anna T. Kitchel. Professor Kitchel explains that the notebook is divided into two parts, which she designates *Quarry I* and *Quarry II*. *Quarry I* contains George Eliot's notes about various scientific and medical matters, historical dates, and several pages of epigraphs for chapters of the novel. *Quarry II* contains plans for the novel, including dates for the action, chapter outlines, "motive, " and outlines of the eight parts. The *Quarry for "Middlemarch"* is reprinted in the Norton Critical Edition of *Middlemarch,* pp. 607–42.

The George Eliot Letters, edited by Gordon S. Haight, were published in 1984–85 by Yale University Press (6 volumes).

Bibliography

Secondary Sources

Reviews of *Middlemarch*

Academy, 1 January 1873, 1–3.
Athenaeum, 7 December 1872, 725–26.
Blackwood's Edinburgh Magazine 62 (December 1872), 743–44.
British Quarterly Review 57 (April 1873), 407–23.
Fortnightly Review, 1 January 1873, 142–47.
Galaxy 15 (March 1873), 424–28.
Spectator, 1 June 1872, 685–87.
Times (London), 7 March 1873, 3–4.

Biographies of George Eliot

Cross, John W. *George Eliot's Life as Revealed in Her Letters and Journals.* 3 vols. Edinburgh: William Blackwood, 1885.

Haight, Gordon S. *George Eliot: A Biography.* New York: Oxford University Press, 1968.

Criticism of *Middlemarch*

Allen, Walter. *George Eliot.* New York: Macmillan, 1964. His essay on *Middlemarch* is reprinted in the Norton *Middlemarch.*

Anderson, Quentin. "George Eliot in *Middlemarch*," *The Penguin Guide to English Literature,* vol. 6. Baltimore: Penguin Books, 1958. Pp. 274–93.

Beaty, Jerome. "History by Indirection: The Era of Reform in *Middlemarch*," *Victorian Studies* 1 (1957–58), 173–79.

———. *"Middlemarch" from Notebook to Novel: A Study of George Eliot's Critical Method.* Urbana: University of Illinois Press, 1960.

Bennett, Joan. *George Eliot: Her Mind and Her Art.* Cambridge: Cambridge University Press, 1948.

Daiches, David. *George Eliot: "Middlemarch."* London: Edward Arnold, 1963. A detailed, chapter-by-chapter reading of the novel.

Edwards, Lee R. "Women, Energy, and *Middlemarch*," *Massachusetts Review* 13 (1972), 223–38. Reprinted in the Norton *Middlemarch.*

Ellmann, Richard. "Dorothea's Husbands," *Golden Codgers: Biographical*

Speculations. London: Oxford University Press, 1973. Pp. 17–38. Reprinted in the Norton *Middlemarch*.

Feltes, N. N. "George Eliot's Pier-Glass: The Development of a Metaphor," *Modern Philology* 67 (1968), 67–71.

Haight, Gordon S. Introduction to *Middlemarch*. Boston: Houghton-Mifflin, 1956.

Hardy, Barbara. *The Novels of George Eliot*. London: Athlone Press, 1959.

———, editor. *Middlemarch: Critical Approaches to the Novel*. London: Athlone Press, 1967. A collection of eight useful essays.

———. *Particularities: Readings in George Eliot*. London: Peter Owen, 1982. A book devoted mostly to *Middlemarch*.

Harvey, W. J. Introduction to *Middlemarch*. Baltimore: Penguin Books, 1965. A good general introduction.

Kettle, Arnold. "George Eliot: *Middlemarch*," *An Introduction to the English Novel*, vol. 2. London: Hutchinson, 1951. Pp. 171–90.

Leavis, F. R. *The Great Tradition*. London: Chatto and Windus, 1948.

Showalter, Elaine. *A Literature of Their Own*. Princeton: Princeton University Press, 1977. A sensitive, enlightening study of George Eliot and other women novelists.

Swinden, Patrick, editor. *Middlemarch: A Casebook*. London: Macmillan, 1972.

Index

The nature of this book is such that to index thematic material would be self-defeating: "reform," "sympathy," "thought," some form of the verb "to do," for example, appear in some form on almost every page. The same is true of the major characters in *Middlemarch*. This index, therefore, is limited (1) to George Eliot's works, excluding *Middlemarch*, and (2) to other writers and thinkers mentioned in the text. The best index to thematic matters I have considered might well be the list of chapter titles, which appears on page vii.

About the Author

Bert G. Hornback is a professor of English at the University of Michigan in Ann Arbor. Among his books are four on Charles Dickens: *"Noah's Arkitecture": A Study of Dicken's Mythology* (1972), *"The Hero of My Life": Essays on Dickens* (1981), *Our Mutual Friend: An Annotated Bibliography* (with Joel J. Brattin, 1984), and *Great Expectations: A Novel of Friendship.* He is also the editor of the Norton Critical Edition of *Middlemarch.*

Hornback is the former director of the Great Books Program at the University of Michigan, director of the Center for the Advancement of Peripheral Thought, and the founder of the Society of Bremen Scholars. He spends most of his time teaching undergraduates, and has been honored four times by the University of Michigan for his excellence in the classroom and as an Honors academic advisor.